The Search for Hannah Lea

Ben Emison and Jerry Branscum

Acknowledgements

Special thanks to Betty Branscum, Denise Hall, Sara Branscum, Sally Harrison, Jo Ann Means, Karon Rudibaugh, Alan Gold, and my wife, Jan Emison, who endured my frustrations.

If people get the impression that Ben and Jerry needed lots of help, that is just fine.

Chapter 1
Second Thoughts

Sam Dallas knew exactly why he had decided to leave the U.S. Army after twelve years of service. He was scared. Sam was not afraid of the search and destroy missions he helped plan and execute; that was his job and he had worked hard to gain the respect and confidence of the officers and men he served with. Sam had completed Special Forces training and was rated expert on several weapons. Sam was also fluent in the Spanish language and this made him very popular with the Latino recruits. It was probably instrumental also in Sam being selected to undergo several hundred hours of total immersion lessons in Arabic. He got high marks from his Arabic instructors but was frustrated with the many different dialects spoken.

What Sam was afraid of was the uncertainty of the situation two years down the road when roughly ninety percent of the U.S. and NATO forces were scheduled to leave Afghanistan. When the new U.S. President had announced the build-up of forces in Afghanistan in 2009, he announced in the same speech that the majority of U.S. and NATO forces would be leaving in 2014.

Sam knew that a small contingent of U.S. forces would remain in the country to train and advise Afghan soldiers. Sam wanted no part of being involved in a caretaker role. The Afghans were not a homogenous people who spoke the same language and shared the same beliefs. There were many different dialects, perhaps only ten percent or less could read and write, and corruption existed at all levels, starting with the President of the country. If that wasn't bad enough, you could add to it the fact that the Taliban had succeeded in infiltrating the Afghan forces with "sleeper Taliban trained moles" who would eventually erupt and start shooting the loyal Afghans and American advisers in he back.

It was still a tough decision to make. Sam was only eight years away from qualifying for a twenty year pension. Then Sam thought "Nonsense! I'm reasonably intelligent, speak three languages, and I know how to supervise people. I also have some old friends out there who can help steer me in the right direction. I'm going to bail out of this mess, I'm going to spend some time seeing my own country and then I'll start looking for a job. Screw it!"

Sam first told Captain Spivey about his decision. He knew the Captain would try to talk him out of leaving, so he listened patiently to the Captain's speech and was respectful but adamant. "Sir," said Sam, "one of the most important things I learned from you and Captain Brown is that once you have decided on a strategy, you stick with it." The Captain waited a minute to see if Sam had anything else to say and then laughed.

"Well said, Master Sergeant Dallas. I will miss you and this particular part of the U.S. Army will miss you. Speaking of Captain Brown, he gave me instructions that should you ever decide to leave this honorable institution, you should be given his phone number with instructions to call him as soon as you are released. Captain Spivey wrote a phone number on a piece of paper and said, "The little captain" is now a senior agricultural analyst with the CIA and is in Oklahoma City finishing up a doctorate thesis that has something to do with 'the coming crisis in world food supplies'. Apparently it's a possibility he alluded to in his master's thesis nine or ten years ago. Very few people believed it at the time but today it's much more likely. Anyhow, you are hereby ordered to call him!"

Sam gave a little salute, said "Yes sir!" and stood up. The Captain stood up and said, "Check in with Sergeant Nash over at the Colonel's office and he will get the process started. I'll let him know you are on your way". This time it was the Captain who initiated the salute and Sam realized that was out of sincere respect on the Captain's part.

The process of getting Sam back to the U.S. was expedited as Sam had over a month of accumulated leave time coming and also because the Army did not want a "short timer" giving less than 100 percent attention on a sensitive mission. Two weeks later Sam was on a plane headed for the USA and he was feeling right good about his decision.

Sam went through the discharge process at Fort Benning, Georgia, signed a few dozen papers, collected a check for his back pay and unused leave time that he was due and was declared a U.S. civilian. There were plenty of regrets but also a feeling of freedom and an anticipation of seeing more of his home country.

Sam caught a bus to Atlanta, checked into a motel,

and contemplated his new life as a civilian. Most of Sam's savings were in a bank in Northern Mississippi and with the cashier's check he had received from the armed services bank in Afghanistan plus his final discharge check from the Army, Sam's total savings amounted to just under $40 thousand. He planned to buy a pickup truck with a camper and to start seeing the country and would start seriously looking for a job when his savings got down to under twenty thousand dollars.

Sam was at peace with himself, had no regrets about his decision to join the army that he had made when he was twenty years old. Prior to that time he had planned to buy his father's farm equipment and farm the land in Mississippi that his father had been renting. That plan fell through when their landlord sold the farm to another farmer who planned to farm the land himself.

Sam's father had offered to pay Sam's college tuition and other expenses but Sam knew that his father and mother would exhaust most of their savings if he agreed to that. Sam's father's health had deteriorated rapidly following his retirement and he died before Sam's first three year enlistment had been completed.

Sam had helped his mother move to a retirement home in Hardy, Arkansas, where she and her sister Martha lived for several years before she passed away. Sam thought that he would swing by Aunt Martha's place in Arkansas and spend at least a few hours with her. He remembered her as an attractive woman, always nicely dressed and who had never failed to bring him a toy when he was small or a nice shirt or other present when he was in high school.

Sam was not aware of any of his close friends who he

attended high school with who still lived where he had grown up. The only exception was Daryl Black, whose skin color was as black as his name. The two had met when the Dallas farm bull had broken out of his pasture, traveled a couple of miles south and broke into the Black family farm, just to see if any of the neighbor's cows were in season.

Sam's father had apologized for his stupid bull's behavior and told Mr. Black that he would return the next day with tools and material to repair the gate and the fence.

When Sam and his father arrived at the Black's farm the next day, a boy Sam's age introduced himself as Daryl Black and said he would help them with the fence fixin'. Daryl was in the eighth grade, the same as Sam but went to a different grade school. Next year he would be in the same high school as Sam. Daryl asked Sam if he had a horse. When Sam replied no, Daryl said, "I have two horses. You come down here Sunday after church and we'll go for a horse ride."

Sam had not seen Daryl since their last baseball game in the district tournament their last year in high school. Sam played first base and Daryl was an all district second baseman. Daryl was a big guy who hit with a lot of power and also played a very good second base, scooping up ground balls or turning the double play, he could be counted on. During the district tournament, Sam had hit almost .500 and maybe he got a little bit too confident. When he came to bat in the bottom of the ninth inning, his team was trailing by one run and there were runners on first and third, two men were out and Daryl would be up next, if Sam could get on base. Sam had worked the count up to three balls and two strikes and was sure he would get a good pitch to hit. "Just take a good swing," he thought, "don't try to kill it. Bring in the guy from third and let Daryl win the game." The three-two pitch was a high rainbow, looked to be way outside, and Sam thought there was no way that ball could ever be a strike. The ball dived in toward the plate at the last second and the umpire called it a strike. Game over. His team was done for the season. They were not going to the state tournament and Sam would regret that for the rest of his life.

He had not seen Daryl since. He knew that Daryl had received a four year baseball scholarship at Mississippi State University and was now a successful farmer, producing among other things, some well bred cutting horses. Sam had not received a scholarship offer and eventually had decided to join the army.

After buying the pickup and camper, he decided his first stop would be somewhere in Colorado. It would be midsummer by the time he got there and he would do some mountain hiking before heading to the North Rim of the Grand Canyon. He had heard that you could drive a 4-wheel drive vehicle down into the canyon from the North Rim. If not, he would hike down and camp out. After all he had done plenty of camping out in the army. From the Grand Canyon, he might duck down to Phoenix and Southern Arizona before turning back north towards San Francisco, Oregon and Washington. He would then make a decision about Alaska.

It was still too early for supper, so Sam decided to walk down to a convenience store and pick up a package of chips and maybe a six pack of beer. Sam selected his purchases, stood in line at the counter, as several people in front of him paid for their purchases. When it was his turn, Sam asked if the store was always this busy. The cashier said, "No, but tonight's power ball lottery is expected to hit between $185 and $190 million." "Wow!" said Sam, "that is more money than I could even imagine." Sam paid for his purchase with a $10 bill and received three one dollar bills in change. "Aw, why not?" he said, "Give me three numbers on that power ball jackpot just for the heck of it." Sam put the power ball ticket in his wallet, turned to leave and found himself staring at a pistol. The young man holding the gun ordered Sam back to the counter and ordered the store clerk to open the cash drawer. The robber then said to Sam, "Let me have that wallet!" Sam extended the wallet toward the robber who reached for the wallet and at the same time shifted his eyes back toward the store clerk. The next thing the would be robber knew, he was lying on his back on the floor. Sam's left foot was on the would be robber's right hand, his right foot was on his neck and Sam was telling the villain to "lie still or I might just squeeze your stupid head off."

The police arrived soon and took statements from the clerk, two other witnesses and from Sam. The officer who took Sam's statement and cell phone number asked Sam if he would be available as a witness. Sam said, "Well, actually I'm traveling through. Give me a number and I'll check back with you in a few days." Sam then checked his wallet and made sure his power ball ticket was still there. Sam chuckled at himself as he realized that his chances of winning were maybe one in several hundred million.

The next morning, Sunday, Sam bought a newspaper

to see if any car dealers were open. He quickly figured out that all of them were open on Sunday afternoons and started looking through the advertisements to see if there was anything similar to what he was looking for. Sam found an F-250 Ford pickup with a diesel engine with reasonably low miles and good tires. He agreed on a price and arranged to close on the truck the next morning. By noon on Monday, he had not only closed on the truck, but had found a camper and had it installed. The next stop was at a grocery store where he bought a few groceries, some ice and some kitchen utensils. Sam then entered Interstate 20 westbound and did not stop until he arrived at the Alabama border welcome center.

Sam was welcomed by a half starved black puppy of indeterminate breed that appeared to be looking for a home. No way! Thought Sam, just what I need is a mangy dog to share my camper with. Sam stepped around the puppy and resisted the urge to pet the poor animal. When Sam emerged from the men's room, the puppy was waiting for him and ran along beside Sam as if he was in charge and Sam was the adoptee. Sam opened the passenger side door and the puppy leaped into the truck and laid down on the floor. Sam swore at himself as he took off toward Mississippi. The further he went, the more he realized the extent of his stupidity. Major freaking mistake, Sam thought. Not only did the puppy smell bad, but Sam was pretty sure the dog was infested with fleas, worms and no telling what else. Perhaps he would name the puppy Alabama since that's where he found him. Right now that was the only friend that he had in this great big country. Alabama would make good company, especially when he was hiking over mountains and camping out in the Grand Canyon.

Sam found a small animal clinic in Meridian, Mississippi and ordered the works for his new friend. Shots, worming, shampoo and the vet suggested that Sam leave the puppy overnight. Sam agreed and left, looking for a truck stop and a motel. His fuel indicator still showed over half of a tank full but he was interested in his fuel mileage. After paying for his fuel, he walked past a newspaper stand whose headline said that the winner of the power ball still had not shown up. Sam purchased a paper and began to get excited as the article stated that the winning ticket had been sold at a convenience store in downtown Atlanta. He then checked into a nearby motel and began to read further in the article before pulling out his ticket to check the numbers. He could not believe his eyes. The very first number on his ticket matched the numbers in the paper. He felt a tightening in his throat and could feel himself sweating. He read the numbers again and then a third and finally a fourth time. He read a little further and saw that the jackpot was estimated to be $186 million and that there was only one winner according to the lottery officials. Sam's heart was still pounding. He laughed at himself, thinking the former "ice water in his veins" special forces Master Sergeant was shaking in his boots and probably the number in the paper was a misprint anyhow. "Slow down!" Sam thought, "Think it through." It was already two or three hours past closing time in Jackson and he would not be there until mid-morning the next day.

Looking around the room, he found telephone Yellow Pages for Jackson and looked first in the L - for lawyers before checking the A - for attorneys. One small ad caught his attention. Ellen Morgan, Attorney tax problems, strategies, and estate planning. Perfect, Sam thought. He would call her at nine o'clock the next morning, pick up Alabama and head for Jackson. He checked the numbers one more time but still thought there might be some mistake.

Sam called Ellen Morgan's office at 8:59 a.m. and was surprised at the quick answer from Ms Morgan's assistant. "I may have a huge tax problem," Sam said, "and would like an appointment with Ms. Morgan late this morning, if possible. "Nothing is available this morning, sir, but Ms. Morgan has an opening at one o'clock." "Perfect" Sam said, "I'm coming in on I-20 from Meridian and need directions please." The directions were simple. Sam picked up Alabama and was on the road. He had to force himself to concentrate on driving, rather than worry about the lottery prize. At 12:55 p.m. he was greeted by a young woman who said, "Come in Mr. Dallas. Ms. Morgan said to show you right in."

Ellen Morgan, Attorney at law, was an attractive African-American woman maybe forty-five or so and just a little on the plump side. "Tell me about your serious tax problem", she said. "Actually", Sam said, "it's a lot more than just a tax problem. I think I may have won 186 million dollars." He pulled out his wallet and handed the lottery ticket to Ellen, along with the article in the newspaper from the previous day. Ellen looked at the ticket numbers and the winning numbers as reported in the newspaper and said, "Mr. Dallas, sign the back of your winning ticket and write down your home address, telephone number and your Social Security Number." "I don't have an address, Ms. Morgan, I just got discharged from the U.S. Army four days ago. I only have a cell phone."

"That will do fine. May I call you Sam please? You can call me Ellen. It's going to take some time to get this all sorted out. I haven't handled a lottery win this big, but I handle some very large estates and have access to some of the best investment advisers in the country from both a safe investment standpoint and from a yield standpoint. I charge 200 dollars an hour for my services, but I do not collect kick-backs or commissions from any investment institutions that I recommend. In fact, I don't recommend investments in any institution that pays commissions."

"Agreed," said Sam.

Ellen pushed a button and said, "See if you can get Marvin Bates on the line for me. Tell him it's a bit urgent." She turned back to Sam and said, "Marvin Bates is the Director of the Mississippi Lottery Commission. We are both personal and business friends and we will try to handle as much as possible from this office and therefore keep this as confidential as possible. We will try to avoid the publicity and harassment you would get from the hundreds of agents, brokers, sharks and con men who want to sell various types of investments." Sam was beginning to like what Ellen Morgan was saying.

"While we're waiting for Marvin Bates to call back, I'll explain the process to you. Marvin will verify the validity of your ticket and will call the Lottery Center in New York. If there are no other winners who would share equally in the payoff, a team of three Lottery executives will fly out on an executive jet to verify that this is indeed the winning ticket. They have the ability to analyze that ticket and assure that it is valid. Once the validity is assured, they'll calculate your tax liability and transfer the funds electronically to the banks that you have designated. This can be accomplished in as little as forty-eight hours."

Ellen's phone buzzed and Maggie's voice said, "Marvin Bates on line one." Ellen picked up the phone and said, "Good afternoon, Marvin, I'm about to make your day more interesting. I have a gentleman in my office who wants to put a document in your hands."

"Let me clean up some details, Ellen, and I'll see you in your office in about an hour."

Ellen hung up the phone and said, "Marvin won't take your ticket, but he'll verify it and give it back to you. You'll have to keep possession of it until the top executives from New York fly out and make the disbursements after the final verification."

Marvin Bates wasted no time in verifying Sam's ticket. He then asked Ellen if he could use her other office to call the National Lottery Office. Ellen said that he could use her office and that she and Sam would wait in the other office.

When they walked into the vacant office, Ellen held out her hand and said, "Let me be the first to congratulate you, Sam, you are a very wealthy man." Sam was speechless and thought he might cry. Instead he decided to take Alabama a drink of water and let him run around outside for a while.

When Sam returned from watering Alabama, Ellen was still in her office writing on a yellow pad. "This is what I'm recommending, Sam. Your cash settlement after taxes will be around $80 million. I think you should put half into the top two banks in the world. I believe you should put the other $40 million into the top five banks here in the South, one of which is right here in Jackson. Over the next several years, you should strive to move at least one half of your estate from cash and securities into farm land and prime real estate. Both pay better returns and are safer in the long run.

Chapter 2
Ellen Morgan

Marvin Bates finished his phone conversation and rejoined Sam and Ellen. "Closing will be Thursday morning at 9:30 at the Jackson Federal Bank. The three executives from the National Lottery Headquarters will arrive Wednesday evening. I'll collect them at the airport, take them to dinner and we'll meet you and Mr. Dallas at the bank. I'll arrange to have a private secure room at the bank and will have the necessary computers, printers, etc. available, so that you can transfer the funds from the Lottery bank account into Mr. Dallas' accounts." Marvin shook hands with Sam and said, "You are a very lucky man, Mr. Dallas and you made a very good choice when you hired Ellen as your attorney and financial advisor. I get my advice from Ellen also."

"That's true," said Ellen, "but Marvin doesn't pay me. He does, however, send me some business from time to time."

Ellen and Sam returned to Ellen's office and she spent more time explaining the investments that she was recommending for Sam. "My gentleman friend, Charlie Wong, is one of the top investment advisors in the world. He publishes a monthly newsletter and sometimes upgrades it each week by e-mail, if necessary. He's also on the staff of the largest investment bank in New York City. He flies back here whenever he can for the weekend and sometimes I meet him in New York for the weekend. The reason I'm telling you all about Charlie Wong is that all of the banks that I'm recommending to you use Charlie as an investment advisor. He meets with their chief investment officers regularly and calls them when he believes a change in investment strategy is warranted."

Ellen then suggested they close up shop and have dinner at a nearby steak restaurant. "It's a very old Jackson landmark, not a lot of frills or fancy decor, just some of the best steak in the South." During dinner Sam asked Ellen why she had decided to open an office by herself, rather than join an established firm.

"Oh, I did join a firm," Ellen said. "There was a six attorney firm, not far from where my office is now, that hired me out of law school. Four of the original attorneys had agreed to take on a young attorney and let them become familiar with their practice over a few years and then let the young attorney buy their practice at an agreed upon price. The only one who followed up on that decision was Wendell Lowenstein, who hired me right out of Ole Miss and helped me prepare for the bar exam. So, I became the seventh attorney in the office. It worked out well for me, because I was able to get experience in other disciplines than just tax and estate planning."

"On Friday afternoons all six of them disappeared into the conference room and played poker all afternoon. If one of their clients had an emergency, I handled it for them."

"My only problem with the six old men was the first day I started, the oldest and most senior attorney took me to the little kitchenette area and began to show me how to make coffee, just the way they liked it. I told him I was a tea drinker and had no interest in learning how to make coffee. Whatever procedure they had used in the past for making coffee would have to continue. I then told him I would be glad to do my part in helping to keep the kitchen clean just like everyone else. I then walked back to my office. When I came in the next morning, Wendell asked if I had finished making the coffee. Then he doubled over laughing and said, 'they voted on whether or not to retain my services and that I won five yeas to one nay.' Wendell stayed around for two years and helped me more than any other person ever did in my law career."

"Wendell also helped me buy my house. The house was on a corner lot in the most exclusive neighborhood in Jackson. The previous owners had allowed it to run down and had put the house up for sale. Wendell had put in a bid for the house on my behalf and had hired an architect to draw up plans for a renovation. The architect outdid himself on the drawing and Wendell convinced the committee that they had no grounds whatsoever to reject my offer. Later on Wendell helped me buy the building where my office is located. I really owe a lot to that funny old man."

Ellen checked her watch and said it was time for her to go home. When they walked outside, she told Sam where a good motel was located and also told him the restaurant across the street from the motel was very excellent.

When Sam arrived at the office, Ellen told him she was getting his accounts set up and getting some checks printed at Jackson Federal Bank. "Marvin called and said the closing is tomorrow at 9 o'clock, instead of 9:30 at the Jackson Federal Bank." Then she said, "Sam, if you go straight up this street, just across the Interstate there is an RV dealer, in case you want to upgrade from that piece of junk out there in my parking lot."

"What do you mean, piece of junk? If I trade my camper in now, I'll lose at least three thousand dollars on the deal."

Ellen patted Sam on the arm and said, "I'm teasing you, Sam, but you should realize that if you lose three thousand dollars that's less than one half day of earnings you will be receiving from your investments. For a month's worth of your earnings you can probably buy a forty foot diesel powered rig with a queen bed, a small kitchen, a refrigerator, and a bathroom with hot and cold water."

"I'll think about it", Sam said as he walked out the door. "Maybe I'll just sell the camper and keep the truck, it will come in handy for checking out farmland. Sleeping with air conditioning might be very nice."

Ellen triple checked the account numbers, the particular investments, including the exact spelling of the investments. She hoped that the lottery officials were prompt and courteous. Ellen had never handled anything this big and she wanted zero glitches. She knew that Sam was an honorable and decent person. If she did a good job on this, she would have his investment business for a long time. Ellen very seldom invited customers into her home but she felt very strongly that Sam could be trusted and she intended to invite him to dinner at her house that night.

Ellen Faye Morgan was chopping vegetables for a Chinese dish and Sam was nursing a glass of red wine. Sam was really not a huge wine drinker but was thinking that if he was going to be entertaining other rich folks maybe he should learn something about wine and fancy hors d'oeuvres. Sam asked Ellen why she was interested in farmland. That was a subject he understood.

"Because they aren't making any more and the demand for food and fiber is increasing rapidly. This rapid growth in demand for farm products will continue to grow as long as developing economies continue to improve. Both my gentleman friend, Charlie Wong, and my daughter's father are saying that farmland that has access to irrigation water is the best investment in this country."

Sam agreed with the statement but wondered about Ellen's choice of words. "What do you mean about your daughter's father? Are you divorced?"

"No" said Ellen, "we were never married. We were attracted to each other and it just happened."

Sam kept his mouth shut. If Ellen wanted to elaborate he would listen.

"We were in law school together at Ole Miss. We spoke occasionally but were not close. Benjamin Bradford III or "Bennie" as we call him was the unofficial leader of a study group that met in the law library. He was clashing with a professor who liked my answers when he called on me and sometimes complimented me on my answers. So Bennie asked if I would join their study group and give him some tips on how to handle Professor 'Corn Pone' as he referred to him. I said fine, why not? There was another girl in the study group that I got along with very well. It was a fun group and Bennie actually kept us on track when the discussions began to meander."

"Since I lived on the other side of Oxford and rode a city bus to school, Bennie offered to pick me up and take me home in his car. I was attracted to him but knew that a relationship with him would lead to nowhere. One night when he dropped me at home, he tried to kiss me. I tried to hit him, called him a few choice names and slammed his car door on him. The next day he apologized profusely and swore he would be a gentleman. And he was. Three nights later when he stopped in front of my house, it was I who leaned over, put my arms around him and kissed him. For the next several weeks, before Christmas of that year, it was the happiest time in my life. I knew that it could not last forever but I just did not care."

"By Christmas break, I suspected I was pregnant and by spring break I was starting to show. My mother and my aunt had a dressmaking business and during spring break they made me some loose fitting dresses and skirts and I made it through the rest of the semester before anyone knew that I was pregnant. Well, Bennie knew, of course. At first he wanted me to get an abortion and I told him absolutely not. Bennie offered to marry me, but I knew that wouldn't work. Bennie's father was one of the top attorneys in Atlanta and the city of Atlanta was not yet ready to approve of a black daughter-in-law for someone that high in Atlanta society. Plus it would ruin Bennie's chances of ever taking over the largest law firm in Atlanta."

"Bennie supported me financially and my mother

and my aunt agreed to keep the baby until I finished law school, passed the bar exam and got established.

"Hannah Lea was born two weeks before my last year in law school. I nursed her until about two days before I had to return to Oxford. We got her switched over to a formula and I left. Leaving that child was the hardest thing I ever" .... Ellen excused herself and left the room momentarily.

Ellen returned, totally composed and told Sam "We are ready to eat." Over dinner she recounted the key points of Hannah Lea's life, including the fact that she was runner up in the Miss Arizona beauty contest last year. She finished with; "she has finished law school and is now studying for the bar exam. She is a beautiful woman - she got my good looks and her father's brains."

Marvin Bates and the New York entourage walked into the bank on time, introductions were made and the party was shown into a meeting room that Bates had requested. The leader of the New York group introduced himself as Joseph Spinelli and asked if Sam would take a chair to his left and Ellen to his right and began the process.

"Mr. Jamison will sit next to Miss Morgan and he will transfer the funds to the institutions you have designated. Mr. Jackson will observe the entire process and try to keep us on track. Mr. Bates will also observe." Sam handed his lottery ticket to Spinelli, who read the numbers off and Jackson confirmed that those were the winning numbers. Mr. Spinelli then stated that the official award was $186,895,250. "That would be the payoff if Mr. Dallas had elected to receive the prize in twenty annual installments. Instead Mr. Dallas has elected to take a lump sum payment. This is calculated to be the amount necessary to equal the total award if invested at the existing rate of interest. With interest rates at record lows, it is to Mr. Dallas' advantage to take a lump sum award rather than the twenty annual payments. Mr. Dallas, your net award, after federal and state of Mississippi income taxes will be $82,434,620." Spinelli passed out copies of the calculations to every person in the room and then told Sam that he would still have to file federal and Mississippi tax returns. Sam Dallas was almost speechless. Finally he replied, "Ellen will take care of my tax returns."

"Mr. Jamison," said Spinelli," you may transfer the funds according to Ms. Morgan's instructions." A few minutes later, confirmations of the transferred funds began to come in on a different machine. When all of the transfer confirmations were in, Mr. Jamison announced that everything was in order. Bates offered to buy lunch for everybody but Ellen declined saying that she needed to get back to the office.

"Let's see if we can get you some cash," Ellen said to Sam. A bank officer directed them to a senior teller where Sam was issued a debit/credit card and was given a piece of paper with his pin number.

Sam said, "I would like five thousand dollars with five hundred in fives, tens and twenties and the rest in fifties and one hundreds." Sam had no idea why he was withdrawing such a large amount. He reckoned his perceptions about spending money were beginning to change. A celebration was in order. He collected his book of temporary checks and was given the name and number of a Senior Officer who would vouch for his credit worthiness if he wanted to make a large pur-

21

chase.

Sam carried the money and the blank checks in his hand as they walked out the door. "I need something to carry this stuff in," Sam said. "I never had anything before that would not fit in a wallet."

"Maggie ordered you something yesterday, Sam. It's our present to you and it's been a pleasure working with you."

"You should have charged me a commission," Sam said, "instead of your hourly rate. I think you actually earned a commission."

"I'm doing fine, Sam. A deal is a deal and I look forward to advising you for several more years on your investments. I get very good investment information from Charlie Wong and from Bennie. Sam, you don't need to tell a lawyer how to charge for their services. That's the first thing we learn. You and I will do just fine together."

When they returned to Ellen's office and told Maggie that everything went fine, "Shake hands with Mississippi's newest multimillionaire." Sam opened the present that Ellen had told him about and found a nice leather case, smaller than a briefcase but when opened it had places to stash and organize things. Sam's name was on the outside in gold letters and Maggie showed him a flap that when lifted revealed a series of flaps for stashing cash of different denominations. "I really appreciate this," Sam said, "my wallet would no longer hold everything."

Maggie picked up the ringing phone, said "Just a minute, please" and handed the phone to Ellen. A few seconds later Ellen hung up the phone and said, "Two FBI agents are on their way and will be here shortly. The person I spoke with would not say what business they have with me. At any rate, Sam, I doubt that it has anything to do with you."

"I'll wait around, just to see what's going on," said Sam.

The two FBI officers arrived and asked if they could speak to Ellen in her office. The meeting was over within ten minutes. The two agents walked out, nodded to Sam and Maggie as they left, and said nothing.

Ellen walked slowly out of her office, sat down and said, "My Hannah has been kidnapped." Ellen tried to say more but could not. She started toward her office but then turned and went to the ladies restroom. Sam thought he could hear sobbing and perhaps retching sounds. Ellen emerged from the restroom and said, "I don't even know where to begin."

"Did they give you any details?" asked Sam.

"A neighbor woman across the street from Hannah's apartment saw her leave the apartment, and a large bald man picked her up and put her in a black SUV with dark windows and drove off. It happened about five o'clock yesterday and they were not able to get my name and information until this morning. The Phoenix office of the FBI is in charge of the investigation. I'm to communicate with an officer named Monroe and I've been told not to give interviews with anyone."

Ellen asked Maggie to get Bennie and Charlie Wong on the phone for her and to get her reservations to fly to Phoenix. Sam asked if he could go with her and would they be better off chartering a plane.

"Yes, yes", said Ellen.

Ellen spoke again to Maggie. "I'm out of the office until further notice. I'll ask Bennie to send a tax attorney over here. He's done it in the past. I'll speak to him and Charlie Wong both. Wait half an hour and then send a cab to pick me up at my house. Sam, I'll meet you at the airport."

Sam pulled a hanging bag out of his truck that contained his clean slacks and sport shirts and one sport jacket. Sam did not own a suit or a tie. He thought for a minute and then put two pistols in a small bag that contained his clean socks and underwear.

Maggie appeared and gave Sam the address of North American Executive Charter Service and their daily and weekly rates.

"I'm glad you're going with her," said Maggie. "Good luck."

Sam saw a taxi slowing to turn into the parking lot and whistled for Alabama, who had been checking out the shrubs.

Chapter 3
The "Little" Captain

If I say the wrong thing, Ellen will explode, thought Sam. If I say the right thing in the wrong way, she will still explode. Ellen knows she may never see her daughter again and the FBI will tell her nothing. That fact allows Ellen's mind to imagine all sorts of frightening scenarios. The fact that there has been no ransom demand after almost an entire day indicates that someone wants Hannah for something other than money. Does someone want to trade Hannah for a terrorist or other prisoner in U.S. custody? That might be possible but he had been told that it was a firm U.S. policy not to negotiate with terrorists, as that would establish a precedent and put more American lives at risk. However, if the FBI had any inkling that a hostage swap might be a possible motive that could cause them to brief the CIA. If so, there is one man who might be able to find out.

Sam had been instructed to call ex-captain Harold Brown and he would do so right now. The message was short and crisp. "Harold Brown, leave a number and I'll call you back."

Sam had spent hundreds, if not thousands of hours

with Captain Harold Brown and was familiar with the Captain's life story. He knew that Harold Brown had been born Harold Klotze in St. Louis, Missouri. "A mile west of the Mississippi river, a mile south of downtown St. Louis and about forty feet from hell" is how the Captain described the project where he was born.

In 1980 Harold's father was killed in a knife fight when Harold was four. His mother was on welfare, did odd jobs as a waitress or bartender and sometimes did not come home at night.

The nights were frightening because the roaches or silverfish came out of the walls when the lights went out and the noise they made sounded like a small army marching.

What was more frightening was the walk back and forth to school. The school was adjacent to the project, no more than three blocks from home. What made this trek a harrowing experience was the gangs, both black and white that demanded money for crossing their turf. Their turf was defined as wherever they happened to be at the time. Sometimes Harold's mother walked him to school and other times the lady next door walked with him. Some days, if he felt really brave, he would peek out the door and if the coast was clear, he would run a couple of blocks west, out of the project, and then turn south on a street that was marginally safer. Some days he just stayed home from school.

Harold's life improved considerably after his mother died and he moved in with his aunt, Kate. Kate was his late mom's sister and generally nice to Harold. Kate had a sharp tongue and constantly harped about her stupid sister who never should have married that worthless lout in the first place.

Aunt Kate's neighborhood was a huge improvement over the project. It was only a mile or so away from his old home, but well maintained and stable. Even going to school was now a piece of cake, as he could run to school in under five minutes and if the weather was bad, he could get a ride with Gene next door. Gene was a retired army sergeant whose wife worked at the same office as Aunt Kate. Gene had also secured a part time job for Harold at the boxing gym where Gene spent most of his time. Local boxers, both amateur and professional, worked out at the gym as well as professionals from out of town. The gym was clean, well maintained and it was cheaper to train in St. Louis than in the major fight cities such as Las Vegas, Los Angeles, Chicago or the New York City area.

Harold was not carried on the official payroll of the gym, but collected tips from the boxers, trainers, and others at the gym. His main job was to pass out clean towels to the boxers and collect the dirty ones. He also hustled sodas from the drink machines for tips and the manager gave him a couple of dollars, if he wasn't busy.

Gene's function at the gym was to observe and analyze the boxers and try to determine how motivated they were in their training. Sometimes boxers trained with little inspiration, leaving the impression that they might be preparing to take a dive. Gene occasionally placed bets for himself and for the gym owner who wanted his personal bets to remain confidential.

Sometimes when a really good boxer was training, Gene would motion for Harold to come watch. "Watch their feet. They don't dance to be cute, they dance in order to have their feet in the right position. You push away with your lead foot and you push into the opponent with the other foot. That puts more of your weight behind the punch. Also the lead knee bends slightly, the hips pivot to bring more power behind a cross punch (left cross or right cross). Reverse everything, push off with the other foot, let the other knee bend and deliver a cross punch with the other hand."

"If you get into a schoolyard fight, don't let the other guy hit you first. Hit him with a good, fast cross punch, do it again from the other side and then take him down and make a wrestling match out of it. Hang on tight and the principal or someone will show up and stop the fight. Remember that, kid."

For the first time in Harold's life, he was no longer afraid. Aunt Kate fed him well, he slept in a clean bed, had clean clothes to wear and there were no bugs marching around at night.

Harold's feeling of euphoria came to a crashing end when Aunt Kate died. She had just finished her shift where she worked at the Army Records Center, walked outside and collapsed. Kate was taken by ambulance to a nearby hospital where she was pronounced dead.

Harold stayed at Gene's house the next two nights. On the morning of Aunt Kate's funeral, a middle aged couple stopped by Gene's house. The lady identified herself as Judy Brown, a sister of Harold's mother and his Aunt Kate. "My husband, Wilbur, and I own a farm in Oklahoma and I have a restaurant in town. We would like for you to come stay with us." Harold looked at Gene, who nodded his head, sending a strong message that the lady was telling the truth. He began to feel the fear in his stomach, stronger than ever before. He looked back at the lady and she seemed very nice.

Wilbur gave him a little smile. He finally asked, "How long do you want me to stay?" The lady laughed at him but he thought there were tears in her eyes. She leaned over and gave him a little hug and said, "As long as you want to stay." Harold decided to go to Oklahoma, but he was still afraid.

As they drove southwest on I-44, Wilbur was telling Harold that they were on part of the old Route 66 made famous by a song. Harold asked Wilbur if there were still wild Indians in Oklahoma. Wilbur laughed and said that the Indians had not been wild in over a hundred years. Harold felt in his back pocket to make sure his stash was still there. He had over $40 that he had saved and thought that he could run away from Oklahoma if it turned out badly. When they drove through a fairly large town and passed by a bus station, Harold thought he could make his way back and catch a bus back to St. Louis. Maybe Gene would let him stay at his house if he helped pay for the food and stuff. Satisfied with his escape plan, he sat back in the seat and went to sleep.

Harold was impressed with the farm. The house was nice sized with a breeze-way and a carport large enough for the car and a pickup truck. There was a huge barn and a large quonset building that served as a shed for the farm equipment.

Judy told Harold to bring his stuff in first and then "Wilbur can show you the farm, the cattle and the horses. I have to go check on my restaurant and I'll bring us some supper back with me."

Harold couldn't believe the size of his room, the huge queen sized bed and a walk-in closet! Everything he owned had fit into a small suitcase and a small cardboard box.

Harold went back outside and found Wilbur loading some mineral and protein blocks into his pickup. They drove out past the barn to a gate and Wilbur said, "Jump out and I'll show you how the gate works. After I drive the truck through, you can close the gate and make sure that it's latched properly."

Wilbur explained things as they drove slowly down the "turn row" at the end of each field. "The horses have their own small pasture they can graze in and they can go into the stalls in the barn if the weather is bad. I have about three acres of alfalfa hay for the horses and I usually get two cuttings of fescue hay for wintering the cows. The horses are work horses but we ride them some."

They came to another gate and Wilbur said, "Let's stop here and have a look. There's a total of about 330 acres or just over one half of a section. A long time ago, the White River ran through this farm. When it changed course and moved several miles further south it left a half dozen bays where it used to run. Two of the bays cover about sixty acres and are twelve to fifteen feet deep in places, so we have a good amount of water for irrigation. We own the land on both sides of the bays so in effect the bays belong to us. There is plenty of catfish and crappie to catch and some bull frogs to gig, and the land on the other side has lots of deer. Let's drop these blocks off for the cows and have a quick look around. Judy will be back shortly with our supper."

Supper was roast beef, mashed potatoes, gravy and rolls and pecan pie for desert. "I decided we needed a good supper since we didn't have a big lunch", Judy explained. "If you guys don't have anything else to do, we could walk down to the Arnolds' house and introduce Harold to his cousins."

Wilbur was still eating and said to Judy, "You better explain that to Harold."

"Audrey Arnold is Wilbur's first cousin and she and her husband, Pete have two children. Jim is a senior in high school and Sandra is in sixth grade. Wilbur's grandfather, who was also named Wilbur, started out with forty acres and a team of mules and built it up to almost seven hundred acres. Neither of his two sons was interested in farming. Wilbur's father was a minister and Audrey's father taught school. Neither of the old man's sons wanted anything to do with the farm, - probably because the old man was such a hard worker and thought everyone else should work as hard as he did. So, the old man got even with his two 'worthless' boys, as he called them and deeded the land to his two grandchildren. Pete Arnold is a lot like his wife's grandfather. He works a hundred hours a week at times, mortgaged their farm to buy more land and it's worked out very well for them. My Wilbur just did things a bit different. He didn't add any more acres to his land but he just made it almost as perfect as possible and we are very happy with it."

It was less than a quarter of a mile walk to the Arnolds' house. Audrey met them at the door and hugged both the Browns and then Harold and said, "Welcome to Oklahoma, Harold, and you will be welcome at this house any time you want to stop by. This is my husband, Pete. You can call us Uncle and Aunt, if you want to."

Harold shook hands with Pete Arnold and then was told to go out back where Jim and Sandra were shooting some baskets. Jim looked at least twice as tall as he was and Sandra was at least a head taller than he.

Jim was shooting baskets from twenty-five feet out, making most of them, and when he missed he retrieved his ball and dribbled in for a monster dunk. Sandra was shooting free throws and making bank shots off of her misses. Harold tried a few free throws, none of which even came close. Both of the kids were nice and told Harold he could come and shoot with them any time he wanted to.

Harold felt intimidated rather than welcomed and was wondering seriously about Oklahoma, where the girls were bigger and stronger than he and the boys were twice as big.

Back at the Browns' house, Harold took a shower in his own private bathroom and put on new pajamas that his Aunt Judy had bought for him. He liked the fact that he had his own bathroom and a queen sized bed but still wasn't sure about living in Oklahoma. He thought maybe he would pretend to be sick the next day and not go to school. Then when Wilbur and Judy were both gone, he would hitchhike back to the bus station and catch a bus back to St. Louis. Having formulated a plan, he went to sleep.

Wilbur woke Harold up and said, "Judy made some blueberry pancake batter. Get dressed and come eat some pancakes." Harold ate four big pancakes and decided that pretending to be sick might not be very convincing. If school was as bad as he suspected it might be, he would wait another day before escaping back to St. Louis.

"Miss Betty"Crandall had been teaching fifth grade for ten years and that was what she intended to do for the rest of her life, God willing. Judy Brown had called her at home earlier in the morning and forewarned her that she was bringing in a fifth-grader who was afraid of his own shadow and who she suspected had some serious learning problems, so Betty had arranged with the principal's secretary to give Harold two tests to determine at what level he might be. The results of the tests indicated that Harold could not read, even at third grade level. Miss Betty recommended to Judy that Harold do fifth grade over and that he spend the summer learning how to read. She gave Judy a list of fiction books for her and Harold to read during the summer. "Have Harold read with you. He's plenty smart. Cure his reading problem and he will do just fine."

At noon, Harold overheard some guys mocking his St. Louis accent and laughing at him. He heard one say, "The dumb ass is going to have to do fifth grade again." Harold started walking away. He could feel the tears coming and that made him even angrier. One of the guys ran after him and grabbed his shoulder, pulling him around. This time something exploded inside Harold. The boxing lessons from Gene finally kicked in; the forward knee bent slightly, the hips pivoting toward the opponent and the right crosses right at the nose. Then bring in the right foot and you go with the left cross. Take the guy down and hang on until someone breaks up the fight. Sure enough, he heard a voice of authority yelling, "break it up, the fight's over." A hand grabbed his collar and pulled him off the other kid. Harold had to do detention. No more playground time, this suited Harold just fine.

Harold got more boxing lessons that summer. The Arnolds' nephew from Oklahoma City came to visit during the summer vacation. Thomas Scott was a bit younger than Harold but slightly larger. Jim Arnold dug out some oversized boxing gloves (they have more padding and do less damage than the regular size). Jim bought the kids some mouth pieces so they wouldn't lose any teeth and let them flail away at each other.

There was also swimming and fishing in the bays and some all nighters where all the guys camped out, caught fish and gigged bullfrogs.

Perhaps Harold did not realize it at the time, but he had inherited a new extended family and began fifth grade with a new attitude about school and about Oklahoma. Miss Betty made school fun. She had the kids choose a state and then write to that state's Chamber of Commerce requesting information about the state. The students were then required to give a five minute presentation about "their state." Following this, they did a similar project on major countries and the other continents. Miss Betty also assigned a tutor to work with Harold on his reading and mathematics. Amanda Stevens was doing eighth grade work in math, grammar, and history and was bored almost to tears with the fifth grade. By the end of fifth grade, Harold had caught up with most of the other fifth graders and was looking forward to the sixth grade.

Harold lettered in basketball his last two years in high school. He was never a starter but was the first guy in when substitutions were made. He wore elbow and knee pads, dived for loose balls and when left open, he could put the ball in the basket from three point range.

He liked mathematics and economics and during his senior year in high school, he took courses in both those subjects at the local junior college.

Chapter 4
Prince Valiant

Sam paid the taxi driver, attached a leash onto Alabama's collar and had just started into the charter office when his phone buzzed.

"Harold here, Sam, it's good to hear your voice."

"Same here, Captain. I hate to unload a problem on you but I need some help." Sam explained the situation and said, "The fact that there is no ransom demand worries me. Hannah's father could come up with a hefty ransom if that's what the kidnappers wanted."

"I agree, Sam. It does not sound good. Are you heading out to Phoenix?"

"As soon as Ellen gets here. We have a charter plane ready to go."

"If I can find out anything, I'll call you back. Which charter service are you using?"

"North American Executive Charters."

"Sam, if you don't hear from me, have them set the plane down in OK City and I'll meet you there."

Ellen arrived a few minutes later with a carton containing sandwiches and drinks for her and Sam. She appeared tired and worn out. Sam was concerned and said, "I can't imagine what you're going through. I don't have children and I've never been involved in a family situation this serious. I do know that you have to take control of your emotions in order to think clearly."

Ellen exhaled audibly and nodded her head saying, "I will try." She took small bites, chewed deliberately and was able to eat part of her sandwich. She dialed Bennie's cell phone number for the third time. When she had called earlier, he was out of his office and wasn't answering his cell phone. When he answered this time, she asked, "Are you alone?" When he said no, Ellen said, "You better excuse yourself and find some privacy. A few minutes later, Bennie asked, "What's up?"

Ellen gave him the few facts she had and told him she would call him back after she met with the FBI. "I'm going to make sure my plane is available for tomorrow and the weekend", said Bennie. "I'm canceling everything here at the office for today, tomorrow and Monday and you can call me back at home."

Ellen asked if Bennie could send a tax attorney to her office starting Monday and hung up. She had no idea how long it would be for.

Sam proceeded cautiously. He knew that Ellen was very close to exploding and he didn't want to be the target. "The FBI is always the first to get involved in kidnapping cases and they will bring in agents from other offices and try to interview anyone who ever had any contact with Hannah. The one thing they will not do is tell you what they know and risk the chance that you would unintentionally leak it to the press."

"What are you trying to tell me, Sam?"

"I'm trying to say that if they've briefed the CIA, I

have a contact with them and he might be able to find out something that would give you some hope."

"Who is your contact?"

"A former army captain who I served under in Afghanistan, Captain Harold Brown. I just spoke with him a few minutes ago and he agreed to see what he could find out and call back. He also asked if we could stop in Oklahoma City and he will meet us there. He felt sure that the FBI had briefed someone at the CIA just in case there was an international connection."

"That's OK Sam, I appreciate your help. But Hannah is my daughter and I don't want a bunch of volunteers getting in the way of the FBI. Is that clear?"

"Very clear and I agree," said Sam.

Sam's phone buzzed and ex-army Captain Harold Brown said that the CIA had been briefed and that an agent in Los Angeles would meet with him and Sam. "Do you have an extra seat on your plane?"

"Hold on. Let me check with Ellen." Sam told Ellen what Brown had said.

"Absolutely," Ellen said, "I look forward to meeting your ex-captain."

Brown was waiting for them at the Oklahoma City airport, came aboard and introduced himself to Ellen and the flight crew. He gave Sam a hug, looked him up and down and said, "at least you made it home with all your body parts."

Ellen noticed Brown's prosthesis which resembled a pair of stainless steel forceps that served as a left hand.

"I can see why you are no longer in the army," said Ellen. "Sam told me that you had a very promising career in the army had you been able to stay."

"Perhaps," said Harold, "but I fell into something I

enjoy just as well."

"Which is?" asked Ellen.

"Whether or not the world is able to produce enough food and fiber," said Harold.

"I have my doubts about that also," said Ellen. "When we get my Hannah back, I want to discuss that subject with you if possible."

Sam was pleased that Ellen was being gracious with Harold but told Harold of her concern about volunteers getting in the way of the FBI.

"I understand your concern." said Harold. "I've met the man who is going to meet with Sam and me. Frankly, I was very surprised that the 'company' had any information at all and more surprised that they would share it."

"It will be very interesting to see what they have," said Ellen. "I'll meet with the FBI and call Sam when I'm finished."

They dropped Ellen off at the Phoenix airport before flying on to LAX International Airport that served Los Angeles. Sam and Harold made their way over to the main terminal, found the Executive Club and told the doorman that they were meeting with a Mr. Jones. "Right this way, please," came the answer. They were shown into a meeting room with only one person in the room, sitting at the head of the table. He did not offer to shake hands but asked Sam what his interest was in the Hannah Lea kidnapping case.

"I m a friend of her mother," said Sam.

"In what way?" asked Jones.

"Business," said Sam. "She handled a claim for me and has become a very good friend."

Jones turned to Harold and asked, "How did you

meet this man?", nodding his head toward Sam.

"He was part of my search and destroy group in Afghanistan. We served together for two years." Jones asked Sam for his full name and rank and said; "I'm going to share some information with you that might help in your search. This is very sensitive information and if it gets out in the public that the 'company' has anything to do with your quest, heads will roll and I'm not speaking figuratively."

"I fully understand what you are saying. I have been put on notice." said Harold.

Jones opened the file and pulled out a picture of a handsome, well dressed man, apparently Latin, probably in his fifties. "His name is Diego Garcia Cardoso. He is known in this country as Don Diego Garcia Cardoso, which indicates that he is descended from Spanish royalty. Our interest in the man is his involvement in illegal drugs. He is the major supplier of cocaine and heroin to the West Coast of the U.S., including Phoenix, Las Vegas, LA, and other medium and large cities all the way up to the Canadian border. He has a unique method of control and distribution that keeps his hands clean. Enough information has been supplied to the FBI to have them close in on his operations but the Justice Department won't allow the FBI to pursue him. He is one of the top contributors to politicians on the West Coast and in Washington D.C.

"Does he have a preference for either of the major parties?" Sam asked.

"He seems to be very well pleased with the current administration."

Harold Brown then said, "I assume you think there is some connection between this man and Hannah Lea?"

"We have absolutely no proof of that," said Jones. "What we do know is that Don Diego enjoys raping black women. He likes rough sex and sometimes he enjoys literally disfiguring his victim. There is a video CD that you will want to look at. He was caught with his pants down, trying to disfigure a bi-racial Hollywood actress. We also know that one of his top enforcers was seen in the Phoenix area the day Hannah Lea was kidnapped. He and another man were seen in a black GMC Yukon about two hours before the kidnapping occurred. That doesn't prove anything, other than physical presence in the area. We also know that Hannah Lea had been the subject of a major article in the Phoenix Free Press recently, touting her accomplishments and physical beauty."

"Don Diego has homes in LA, Las Vegas and in Jackson Hole, Wyoming. The latter seems to be his favorite for extended visits. It sits up high on a plateau and he has some sixty acres of pasture and some prize Gelbvieh cattle. His private plane flew there from here a few hours after Hannah Lea was kidnapped. There were no witnesses of who boarded the plane or who deplaned in Jackson Hole. The flight plan showed that there were three passengers on the plane named Smith, Jones, and Adams, all identified as employees of Don Diego's company. The plane returned to LA the next morning with only the pilots aboard. There was sufficient time for a vehicle to drive from Phoenix to LA between the reported time of the kidnapping and the departure of Don Diego's plane from LA."

"If Hannah Lea is destined to be a major project of his, she may be getting heroin shots twice a day or more to get her addicted before Don Diego begins his party with her. When he is finished with his women, he gives them to one of his suppliers in Mexico or Central America and they are never seen again."

"Let me remind you one more time, this is all speculation. The evidence against Don Diego does not even qualify as circumstantial. However, if a ransom demand isn't made soon and if the FBI doesn't come up with another suspect, the case against Don Diego grows considerably stronger."

"Don Diego's business cover is his international retail business. He inherited the major onyx quarries and finishing factory in Mexico from his father. Later on he purchased the major European supplier of onyx in Italy and soon after that Don Diego bought a jewelry manufacturing plant in Switzerland. He has combined all three into a very lucrative international jewelry business that also includes expensive women's apparel. He used profits from his drug business to finance his retail business and uses the retail business to launder his drug profits. He is a very astute businessman."

"What is amazing is that Don Diego hates the U.S. with a passion, holds it in utter contempt. He is joined in his hatred of the U.S. by many other well-to-do Mexicans who want to blame Mexico's problems on the United States. They are persuaded that all of Mexico's problems originated when the U.S. took over half their country in the War of 1846-1848. This is preposterous. If Mexico had been colonized by Japan instead of Spain, the entire North American continent would be speaking Japanese. Instead the corrupt feudal system imposed by the Spanish on a peaceful, gentle, hard-working people lives on to this day. Unless you are born to 'somebody' in Mexico there is a little chance of ever getting a decent education. There is a very small cadre of top managers, engineers, and lawyers who run the country. Corruption is a way of life and it doesn't matter which political party is in power. There is a very thin middle class of plant managers, accountants and other administrators and near the bottom are the hourly construction and factory workers who at least have a job. At the very bottom, between forty and fifty percent of the people are either unemployed or under employed, selling Chiclets gum or pencils on the street."

"There is corruption at every level. Anyone who wants to do business in Mexico has to pay a bribe in order to get a business permit and then pay bribes to all of the local authorities to get water, power, and other permits. The huge U.S. retailer, Ray Mart's Discount Stores was roundly criticized for having paid bribes to obtain various business permits. Hell's Bells! Bribes? If you don't pay bribes for permits in Mexico, you don't do business in Mexico. It's that simple. More than likely the little children or the double amputees who sell Chiclets or pencils on a street corner are paying off somebody!"

"The Mexican drug wars have resulted in fifty thousand people murdered in the last five years. For some reason, Mexico is persuaded that all of this is the fault of the U.S. The various police agencies have a corruption rate of almost one hundred percent and this includes the Federales. All of these problems, the poverty, the unemployment, the drug wars, and the corruption are all the fault of the gringos in the north."

"Don Diego and other billionaires, some European, some South Americans and many Americans have reportedly dumped hundreds of millions into the current administration to help with their reelection."

"Who are the other billionaires?" asked Brown.

"There are lots of speculation', said Sam, "and it really doesn't matter, they have convinced a majority of the American voters to vote their way while slowly destroying the middle class that built this great country. My opinion is that within the next two decades there will only be two classes of people in this country, the rich and the poor, just like Mexico."

"If you want to communicate with me," said Jones, "put an ad in the on-line personals of the LA Times and address it to 'Prince Valiant'. If I have something for you, I'll address it to 'Oakie One'. We will refer to Don Diego as 'the solution'."

Jones stood and said "Good day gentlemen" and started for the door. Brown asked quickly, "Do you need 'the solution' alive?"

"Absolutely not" said Jones as he walked out the door.

Brown and Dallas looked at each other for several seconds before they realized that "Prince Valiant" had walked off and left the file on the table. "Now we know why he was wearing gloves" said Sam.

Chapter 5
The Strategy

Sam's phone buzzed as they walked outside the LAX terminal into the sunshine. "Hey, Ellen, this is Sam. How did you make out with the Feds?"

"Terrible, I hope you and Harold had a better day than I did."

"Maybe," said Sam, "We have some information but nothing really firm to go on. It appears that the hunt should start here in LA. Do you want us to send the plane to pick you up?"

"No, there are flights every hour to LAX. See if you can get me a room with a table we can work from."

"Will do, we saw a Hilton and a Sheraton coming in. Is the Hilton OK?"

"Fine, let's plan to eat in my room and get started."

"I'll call you back if there's a problem," Sam said and pushed the end button.

Sam showered and sat down to get his thoughts together. Harold knocked on his door and came in. "Exactly what kind of claim did Ellen settle for you?" Harold absorbed the information Sam gave him in near disbelief. "You mean, you've been a civilian less than a week and you are a multi multi-millionaire?"

"It's my reward for clean living. You knew I was an Eagle Scout didn't you?"

"So was I, but I never fell into anything like that."

"I'll tell you what," Sam said. "You find us a good deal on a nice farm or a cattle ranch. I'll finance it and you run it."

"No thanks", said Harold, "I was only teasing. I'm buying the family farm from my aunt and uncle who adopted me. I have a great job with the 'company' and most of all I'm doing what I always wanted to do and that is Ag Econ research. I get accurate information on everything I'm interested in every week and I couldn't be more satisfied."

"How is your love life, Captain?"

"Sam, I'm no longer a captain and you should learn to call me Harold. To answer your question, it's absolutely perfect. I'm engaged to an old high school classmate. The lady is divorced and she is also getting a PhD degree in mathematics. We're considering writing a book together."

"When's the wedding?"

"As soon as I submit my doctoral thesis. She says she's not going on a honeymoon with me if I'm still working on that."

There was a knock on the door. Sam opened it and Ellen asked if he would order some dinner for the three of them to be delivered to her room. "I want something with some meat gravy and rolls and I also want some red wine and some coffee! I'm totally beat and I'm hungry. Come on over in about twenty minutes."

"Yes ma'am," said Sam and saluted. When Ellen closed the door, Sam said to Harold, "I think we have a new captain."

The guys knocked and entered Ellen's room. "If the FBI knows anything they aren't telling me," said Ellen, "They grilled me for an hour about Hannah's love life and boyfriends. All I could do was give them some names of guys she hiked with and skied with. When she hikes the Grand Canyon, it's all girls except the hike master and he's married to one of the hikers. I told them that Hannah was pretty serious about another law student her first year in law school but the last I heard that's been over with for over a year and the young man is now engaged to another woman."

"They are trying to prepare me for the worst," said Ellen. "They told me the longer this goes on, the less chance we have of ever seeing her again. It's very depressing." She took a deep breath and asked, "What did you find out today?"

Sam picked up the "Jones file" and put it on the table. "This was prepared for us by a Mr. Jones. He told us that the evidence is completely circumstantial but I think he would convict the man if it were left up to him."

Sam first took out the picture of Don Diego Garcia Cardoso, gave it to Ellen, told her his full name, what he did, and that he was a billionaire. He was also known to enjoy rough sex with black women, but did not tell Ellen about the drugs and the suspicion that Don Diego had sold some women to Mexican or South American bordellos, and were never seen again. He gave Ellen all of the info on Don Diego, his vast retail business and his domination of the drug business on the West Coast.

Ellen asked about Don Diego's private jet flying to Jackson Hole. "According to the flight plan, there were

46

two pilots and three passengers on board. There were no witnesses who saw the passengers board. The names of the passengers on the flight plan were listed as Smith, Jones and Adams, all employees of Don Diego's retail business. The plane returned the next day with only the pilots on board.

"So if Don Diego's hoodlums snatched Hannah, then they might be holding her in Jackson Hole?"

"Very possible," Harold said.

"Do you think you can handle the 'rough sex video'?" Sam asked.

"Let's get it over with," Ellen breathed with a sigh.

The very tan Latin man was slowly undressing a beautiful young woman when he sat up and screamed, "You're black! Nigger bitch" he screamed as he hit her with his fist, breaking her nose. The woman managed to get off the bed and ran for the door. The man caught up with her and slammed her back down on the bed. Then he turned, found his trousers and pulled out a knife. He pushed the switchblade button and took a vicious swipe at the woman's neck. The man dived at the woman and missed. The woman picked up a chair for protection and was crying and begging, "Please, please don't hurt me any more".

At that time the door burst open and a huge black man with a shaved head burst into the room. He grabbed the man's arm, took the knife from him and said, "Put your pants on, the cops are on their way here." He then took a roll of bills out of his pocket and threw them on the bed. "That should cover the damage," he said and ushered the attacker out of the room.

"That we were told is Don Diego. Nice fellow." Harold said.

Ellen looked as if she might be ill. She said nothing.

Finally, Ellen asked, "What else do you have?"

Sam held up a piece of paper. "This is the name, address and phone number of a private detective agency. The owner of the agency has been trying to hang something on Don Diego for years. They supposedly answer the phone twenty-four hours, seven days a week. Why don't we get some sleep and call them the first thing in the morning? Bang on our doors and we will be ready when you are."

"Fine," said Ellen. "Let's see where we go from here before we check out. They have a continental breakfast buffet downstairs. If the detective agency can see us right away, let's just get a quick bite and move on out."

"Come on down," was the message from the Jack Downs Detective Agency, imitating just slightly Ellen's Southern accent. "Jack will be here shortly."

A nice Latin lady asked if they would like some coffee. She seemed to be allowing her eyes to linger over Sam somewhat and Sam said, "Please, that would be very nice." Ellen and Harold both declined the coffee offer. When the young woman brought the coffee to Sam, he stood up and introduced himself.

"It's nice to meet you, Sam. I'm Maria."

As Maria walked away, Sam was thinking, yes and she could have played the part of Maria in "West Side Story".

Jack Downs walked in, introduced himself and invited them into his office. Ellen wasted no time. "We are trying to determine if Don Diego Cardoso had anything to do with the kidnapping of my daughter."

"What do you know about her kidnapping?" asked Downs.

Ellen explained what they knew, that the FBI had not uncovered any leads and there was no ransom demand. Downs made a couple of notes and said, "Tell me about your daughter, please."

Ellen handed over a picture of Hannah, said, "she just graduated from law school and was studying for the bar exam." Ellen continued, "She was runner up Miss Arizona last year and recently there was a feature article about her in the Phoenix newspaper."

"I assume the FBI is telling you nothing." Downs said.

"Correct," said Ellen, "and I spent three hours with them yesterday trying to convince them that I know nothing about her love life and if she was very serious about someone, I would be the first to know."

"Why do you suspect Don Diego? asked Downs.

"A man by the name of Jones suggested that Don Diego might be involved," said Harold. "He also said that one of Don Diego's employees was seen near Hannah's neighborhood prior to the kidnapping. Mr. Jones also recommended that we talk to you."

"Did Mr. Jones give you a video of Don Diego and a certain African-American actress?"

"Yes, he did."

"Excuse me one minute", said Downs. He got up and opened a file drawer and pulled out a folder. He sat back down and removed from the file an 81/2 by 11 black and white photo of a very large African-American man. The man was not unattractive and had a very shiny shaved head. "Paul Hastings," said Downs. "He was a reserve center on the UCLA football team. He racked up a lot of minutes as he could play several positions as a lineman and as a line backer. He also went through the MBA program at UCLA with Don Diego. He is very strong, very intelligent, very loyal to Don Diego and very, very mean. Don't give him a second chance!"

Jack started writing on a pad all of the details and time sequence of when Hannah had been kidnapped, when Ellen had been notified and confirmed again that the FBI claimed to have no leads. He asked again about Don Diego's airplane flying again from LA to Jackson Hole, Wyoming, departing a few hours after the kidnapping was reported.

"Don Diego has his own hangar building at the LA airport. That makes it possible to drive cars and trucks into the hangar to load and unload without any prying eyes to know what is going on. That only proves the possibility that Hannah was taken to Jackson Hole. All three passengers remained in Jackson Hole and the pilots flew back empty the next morning." Downs continued, "If there were no passengers returning to LA, one wonders why the pilots did not return to LA immediately. It's less than two hours flight time from Jackson Hole to LA. Perhaps they did not want to unload their 'cargo' until later in the evening."

Jack Downs continued, "If Don Diego is holding Hannah in any of his homes, it would most likely be either here in LA or in Jackson Hole. The other homes Don Diego owns are much smaller and don't have the privacy necessary to hold a hostage."

"The mansion here in LA is enclosed with a twenty foot concrete wall with razor wire on top of the wall. It's possible to fly over it in a helicopter, and count the cars and maybe get an idea of what's going on, if anything."

Downs then added, "If you want to keep Don Diego

occupied with business here in LA, I can help. Don't ask me how, but I'm pretty sure I can keep him here this weekend."

"If I had the cash to keep a couple of sharp anti-monopoly lawyer going over the weekend, I could have a restraint of trade charge against him by next Tuesday or Wednesday. That file cabinet there is full of names, dates, and facts of what Don Diego has done to eliminate his competition."

"If you want lawyers, I can provide lawyers", said Ellen. "I can have lawyers here on Sunday, if you can clear off a large table to work on so they can organize their papers."

"I'm reasonably sure that I can keep Don Diego here in LA this week-end. By Tuesday or Wednesday, we should be able to file a restraint of trade charge against him, but he will probably be able to get a continuance filed before the next weekend and it is very doubtful if there is anything we can do to keep Don Diego away from Jackson Hole the following weekend. Jackson Hole is said to be his favorite escape. Keeping him here this weekend will cost you five thousand dollars."

Ellen looked at Sam and said, "Loan me twenty-five hundred dollars, please." Sam opened his new leather bound carrying case and began to count out money. Ellen removed an envelope from her purse and did the same.

Jack Downs took the money and asked Maria to write out a receipt for Ellen.

Sam said, "I need to see if you can locate two guys who are from LA and may still be here."

"Give Maria their names. If they are still in California, she can probably find them. Sam wrote on a piece of paper, Pedro Tomas Soto and Ismael Murano Lopez. He gave the names to Maria and asked if she could locate them. He added that they had been discharged from the U.S. army several months earlier.

Sam suddenly remembered Alabama and said, "Darn, I forgot about my dog."

"Where is he?" asked Maria.

"At the airport, with the pilots."

"Have them bring him here. There's a runway and a dog house out back. Tell me his name and I'll take care of him."

Maria left the room leaving Ellen, Sam and Harold alone. "I will call Bennie and get him to meet me in Phoenix. If the FBI has nothing new, I will get him going on the monopoly charge. He has plenty of contacts here in LA and should have no problem getting some lawyers here at Jack's office by noon Sunday. It will cost a fortune but Bennie has a fortune."

"Harold and I will fly with you to Phoenix", said Sam. "If Maria can find where my two Latinos are, I want to speak with them."

"What do they do?" asked Ellen.

"Pete Soto alias 'Sparky' Soto is an electronics wizard and Ismael Lopez is a weapons man."

"Do they call Ismael 'Ishy'? Asked Ellen

"No" said Sam. "They call him 'Malo' or 'Muy Malo'."

Maria returned and said, "Here is a number for Mr. Soto. It is a local number and I'm still working on the other one."

Sam stepped outside and punched in "Sparky's" phone number. An angry voice answered on about the sixth or seventh ring. "Yo, mon, what you want?"

52

"This is Sam."

"Sergeant Sam from Afghanistan? I'm not going back there if that's what you want!"

"No" said Sam. "I just need you for a week or ten days but the pay is good."

"How good?"

"It's hazardous duty and it pays $1,000 per day."

"Okay. I start right now."

"Can you meet us at the airport within an hour?" asked Sam.

"Yeah, I only have to clean up first."

"Clean up good, there's a nice lady with us. Do you know where Malo is?"

"Yeah, mon. He is staying in San Diego."

"You think Malo might like some work?" asked Sam.

"Malo would jump through blazing hoops for $1,000 dollars a day."

"Okay, tell Malo to meet us at the San Diego airport three hours from now. We'll see you at LAX as soon as you can get there. Remember to clean up and act nice for the nice lady." Sam gave Sparky the name of the charter company and said "You can leave your car there."

Sam walked over to where Ellen and Harold were waiting for the cab. "We have a communications man and maybe a weapons man." Sam went back inside the agency and asked Maria if she had had any luck finding Lopez.

"Not yet," said Maria, "but I'm still trying."

"Don't bother," said Sam. "Sparky knows his number." Sam thanked Maria again for keeping Alabama and desperately wanted to say something else but all he could think of was "I really appreciate your help."

The cab arrived with one of the pilots and Alabama. Sam introduced Alabama to Maria. The pilot, Harold, Ellen and Sam squeezed into the cab and headed for the airport.

Chapter 6
Los Dos Latinos?

They dropped Ellen off at the Phoenix airport and the pilot immediately requested approval to take off for San Diego. Ellen would wait for Bennie's plane to arrive and then both of them would check in with the FBI for the daily briefing. Ellen was no longer optimistic about the FBI briefing.

Flying on to San Diego, the conversation began about Malo Lopez.

"Yeah man," said Sparky. "He had three Spanish names and was trying to imitate a Latino speaking English with a Latin accent. I knew right away he was not Latino and I asked him who he was running away from. A big mean drug dealer he tells me. So I asked, 'Did you steal some of his drugs?' And he say, 'No mon, I killed some of his people!' I say, No wonder he's so pissed off; good men are hard to find! We became best buds and stayed together all during boot camp."

"He knew his job and did it well," said Sam.

"Absolutely," said Harold. "The man never hesitated when given an order."

"He sure saved my life," said Sparky, "I took a big

round in my right arm, probably a .45 caliber. It broke a bone and severed an artery and I was sure I would die. I was just sitting there in shock watching it bleed. Malo, he put a tourniquet on my arm and then he got on my radio, told the chopper guys where the fire was coming from and after the chopper guys take care of the bad guys, he carried me down to where the chopper sat down and then he went back and got my equipment. One more thing," said Sparky, "he no longer wants to be called Malo. He wants everyone to call him Ismael or Lopez. He has a new Latina lady. She makes him go to church with her and they get married pretty soon."

"How did he get the three Latin names in the first place?" asked Sam. "He was obviously a gringo and everyone knew that."

"There was a drug war going on in L.A. Malo was a bodyguard and a hit man for one of the drug bosses. He kills some of the other drug boss' people. Then his own boss was bringing a huge load of drugs through Central America and they were ambushed by the other L.A. gang. Everyone was killed except Malo. He was hurt, but not bad. He laid there until it was dark and traded wallets with the guy that fell on him. The other guy was Latin and both he and Malo had never been arrested and never been fingerprinted. It took Malo six weeks to make it back to the U.S. He lost forty pounds, grew a beard, dyed his hair and beard black and got some dark contacts. He stayed in San Diego and never went back to L.A.

"I'm glad Lopez has been tamed and housebroke," said Sam. "We'll do our best not to blow his cover.

Lopez was waiting for them in San Diego. He embraced everyone and spoke near perfect Spanish to

Sam and Sparky.

"Your Spanish has improved," said Sam.

"I'm staying with a nice Latina lady and we're planning to get married."

"You seem very happy and prosperous," said Harold. "If we could put Don Diego in jail or make him disappear, that would improve your life even more."

"Definitely," said Lopez. "He is the man who wants me dead."

"That's why we are here," said Sam, and he began to explain the kidnapping of Hannah Lea and that so far Don Diego was the prime suspect. "We think he is holding Hannah at his chalet in Jackson Hole, Wyoming. We're trying to keep him busy in L.A. until we find out for sure where Hannah is. We need you to get us some weapons and ammo and we need you to help us for a week or so. The pay is $1,000 per day."

"How many people do you have?" asked Lopez.

"We have four, counting you." I think it will be over with by a week from tomorrow at the latest."

"Do you have a list of what you need?" asked Lopez.

"Two .45 caliber machine guns, a .45 automatic pistol, and a good sniper's rifle with a very good scope and a silencer."

"Wow!" said Lopez . "The rifle alone with the silencer will cost three, maybe four thousand."

"I'm not surprised," said Sam. "I would also like an explosive pack with a timer and detonator."

"How powerful do you want it?" asked Lopez.

"Not very," said Sam, "maybe like six sticks of dynamite." Sam then asked Lopez what weapons did he own personally?

"A thirty-eight pistol with a short barrel, a pump

shotgun, and a thirty caliber army carbine."

"We're going to need an SUV with dark windows to haul this stuff in and I need to find a bank and a restaurant, in that order."

The cashier at the airport branch of a San Diego bank checked Sam's bank card and counted out ten thousand dollars in one hundred dollar bills. Sam gave nine thousand dollars to Lopez and said, "That should cover it. Let's get some lunch now and then we'll get you a vehicle."

They had lunch, found a van for Lopez, who would begin filling Sam's order immediately. Lopez said that he and his lady would come back to the airport later and pick up his car.

Back in L.A. the three got a room at the Hilton for Sparky so that they could get together later. Sam called the Jack Downs Detective Agency to see if anything was going on. Maria answered and said, "Yes, Sam, hang up and turn your TV on to Channel 5!

Sam turned on the TV and the scene on Channel 5 was showing smoke coming out of the Latin Pizzaz store on Rodeo Drive in Hollywood. The TV announcer was doing her best to make a major catastrophe out of the incident. The crowd was enabling. One fire truck was pumping several hundred gallons a minute of water into the building. People were rushing out of the building, trampling those who had fallen, while others were scooping up merchandise, filling their pockets and purses.

The announcer said there were conflicting reports regarding the cause of the fire and that a spokesperson for the Latin Pizzaz Company said it was too early to estimate the dollar amount of the damage or how long the store would be closed.

Sam watched a few more minutes and called the Detective Agency again. This time Jack answered the phone himself. Sam asked Jack if he had heard from Ellen.

"She called a few minutes ago. The FBI had little more to add to what they had told her yesterday. She also said that Hannah's father would be here tomorrow afternoon with one other attorney and they would probably have two more attorneys by Monday."

"I would like to meet with you as soon as possible," said Sam.

"How much time do you need?"

"Thirty minutes, maybe less."

"I'll pick you up outside your hotel at 6:30 A.M. tomorrow."

Sam called Harold and asked if he could grab Sparky and come over to his room. "Ask him to bring his computer."

"You want to see if there is a message from Prince Valiant, do you Sam?"

"How did you guess? I know it's only been one day but I'm anxious to know if the Prince is going to keep feeding us information."

When the guys arrived, Sam asked Sparky if he could plug his computer in here at the hotel.

"Of course, man, you are no longer in Afghanistan. Modern hotels have 'cloud'. You don't need to plug in." They did need however, to open an account with the L.A. Times in order to access and leave messages in the Personals section. There was one message from Prince Valiant to Oakie One which read, "No solution on slopes in Jackson Hole but a nurse is on the scene."

"Answer it, please," said Sam. "Tell him 'thanks for the ski slope update' and sign it Oakie One."

"Ellen hasn't called," Sam said, "But Jack Downs spoke with her and she had nothing new to report from the FBI, but she did tell Jack that Hannah's father would be here tomorrow to start working on the monopoly or restraint of trade suit."

Sam then turned to Harold and said, "When Lopez gets here with the stuff, I would like for you and him to drive it through to Jackson Hole, scout out the area and see if you can put together a plan of action."

"Okay," said Harold. "No problem."

Sam turned to Sparky, "Do you know of any reason why Lopez would not be able to go along with Harold?"

"I don't think there will be a problem. Lopez doesn't work nine to five. He spends a lot of time sourcing and inspecting guns for the store and he is in very tight with his boss."

"I'll see you guys at breakfast downstairs. Seven-thirty okay?" Sam checked his watch after the guys left. It showed 6:30 p.m., but that was Central Time so that it would only be 4:30 here in L.A. He would get a cab and go check on Alabama at Jack Down's office. If Maria was still there, that would be nice also. Sam freshened up a bit and headed downstairs, feeling like a man with a purpose.

Sam walked into Jack Down's office, said hello to Maria and said he just wanted to check on his dog. Maria went and opened the back door and returned with Alabama hot on her heels.

"Hey boy," said Sam. Alabama wagged his tail at Sam but followed Maria to her desk and laid down by her feet.

"I could sue you for alienation of affections."

Maria laughed and said, "Well, I did play with him at lunchtime. He is pretty smart. Did you have a hard day?" Maria asked.

"It wasn't all that hard or all that long. We flew to Phoenix, then on to San Diego, had a nice lunch and flew back here."

"Are you still at the Hilton?" Maria asked.

"Yes, and I suppose I should be getting back. If you will call me a cab, I'll leave you alone so you can finish your work."

"I can drop you off, I live out that way. Give me just a few minutes to finish up."

Maria's car was an eight year old sport coupe with a stick shift and Maria took it through the gears skillfully. "I need to stop at the tea store, if you are not in a big hurry. Do you like tea?"

"Iced tea is nice on a hot day."

Maria laughed and said, "I'll have them make us a cup of hot tea that you might like."

I could learn to like hot tea, if that's what it takes. She has a nice voice, a very nice laugh, and she is beautiful. When Maria stopped in front of the Hilton, Sam said, "Thanks for the tea and the ride. I would really like to have dinner with you sometime, if you are not attached to someone else."

"Could you handle some Mexican seafood tomorrow night? It's a bit spicy."

"Spice is okay."

"I'll make reservations for us and call you, Sam."

Sam, Harold and Sparky had dinner in the Hilton dining room. Afterward, Sam complained of being road weary and said he was calling it a night. Harold agreed saying he was "beat" also. Sparky said he was going for a walk.

Sam and Harold got on an elevator and Sam said, "I need some advice if you have a few minutes." They entered Sam's room and Sam said, "I'm meeting with Jack Downs in the morning and I'm going to see if he can put together another operation for us." Sam continued, "according to Jack Downs, only two of Don Diego's residences are large enough and private enough to keep a hostage. One is the walled monstrosity here in L.A., and the other one in Jackson Hole. I'm going to see if he can organize a break-in into the walled estate here in L.A. with some off duty police or fake police to make sure that Hannah is not there. What do you think?"

"If Jack has enough cop friends, it might work. They would need to look authentic and be able to recite some city ordinance that states that all of the rooms in a house that is attacked must be inspected to make sure that the house is safe. Downs hates Don Diego. If he thinks there is a possibility of making it work, he will go for it."

"My thoughts exactly," said Sam.

Chapter 7

Sam was standing in front of the Hilton at 6:25 a.m.
Jack Downs drove up at 6:30 in a black SUV with
dark tinted windows. Sam got in the vehicle and Jack
drove around behind the hotel, backed into a parking
space and lowered the window on Sam's side, about
halfway. "I thought maybe I was being followed, but
apparently not. What's up, Sam?"

"Nice job there on the Rodeo Drive," Sam said.

"Yeah," said Jack, "Don Diego was probably up until
midnight trying to quash the TV coverage and today
and tomorrow's newspaper coverage. He wasn't successful, there are more stories in today's paper and
there will be still more in tomorrow's Sunday paper.
Don Diego will be trying to quell the public relations
disaster the entire weekend."

"I want to know if it's feasible to break into Don
Diego's walled house here in L.A. with an old SUV full
of explosives. After the explosion, I want a half dozen or
more fake cops to burst in, strong arm their way
throughout the house and check every room to see if
there's a hostage. What do you think?"

"It's not something I can do with my regular guys. I would have to go through an intermediary. When would you like it done?"

"Tuesday night."

"I'm not even sure I could come up with the explosives by then."

"I have some coming," said Sam.

"Do you have any other objectives, other than making sure the girl isn't there?"

"Yes," said Sam, "if there's any evidence that could be left behind that would indicate that one of Don Diego's drug distributors was to blame for the attack, that might help create a civil war, especially if it's a distributor who Don Diego doesn't trust."

"I will check with someone," said Jack. "There is one guy who hates Don Diego more than I do and he has friends who could make it happen. I'll try to meet with him later today. First, I have to get the attorneys started on the other project. There will be two in my office today and three tomorrow afternoon. On Monday they move all their stuff to a different office and if everything works out, a lawsuit against Don Diego will be filed on Tuesday or Wednesday."

Sam considered that for a moment and asked, "On whose behalf are they filing?"

"Six different merchants who have been adversely affected by Don Diego's unfair business practices will be the plaintiffs. A law firm that represented some of the merchants will file the case. It will be a very serious case against Don Diego. Ellen's friend Bennie is giving this case a new life."

"Let me know what you find out about the other possibility we discussed," Sam said.

Jack Downs dropped Sam off at the front of the hotel. Before entering, Sam punched Ellen's cell number.

"How are you doing, Sam" Ellen asked. "There is nothing new here and the FBI is running out of people to question. It's very discouraging to me. All I can do is pray and I do that constantly."

"I understand; it has to be very frustrating to you. Jack Downs struck back yesterday and that will keep The Suspect in town for a few days. Bennie is getting organized at Jack's place and they think they might have a case to file by Tuesday. We're trying to put together another operation. I won't go into it now. Also, Harold and Sparky's buddy Lopez will be heading out to Wyoming, probably by Monday morning."

Jack Downs called Sam at 2:50 p.m. and said, "Get a cab and go up to the Am Vets club. It's about four miles up on the same street as the Hilton. Do you still have some army ID?"

"Yes," said Sam.

"I'll be along shortly."

Sam followed the instructions, showed an army I.D. card and was allowed into the club. He ordered a Coke and paid for it as Jack Downs walked by and motioned for Sam to follow. They entered a room with a poker table, empty of any cards or chips. An old man, at least seventy, Sam thought, well dressed and well groomed, was seated at the table. A younger man, holding an electronic device said to the older man, "It's clean," and walked out of the room.

The old man began to talk. "Four police cars with radios and all the gear, eight bona fide cops can do what you are asking. They will all have a legitimate reason to be in the area. They will be the first police responders and will search every room in the house and with any luck, they'll be leaving as a dozen other police cars and fire trucks arrive on the scene."

"You are to supply an old, four wheel drive vehicle with a chrome dealer identity on the back. The dealer identity has to be this one." He handed Sam a card with an auto dealership name on it. "You are to acquire the vehicle by noon Monday and have it at this address," said the old man as he handed Sam another card. "It used to be a gas station but now they do repair work."

"It will cost you $50 thousand and that's a bargain."

"It will be sometime Monday before I can get cash," said Sam.

"Jack will give me his check to hold. Give the cash to Jack and I'll catch up with him later. Bring the explosives and timer with the vehicle when you drop it off on Monday."

The old man stood up and walked out of the room without offering to shake hands.

Sam turned to Jack, "Do you think it will work?"

"I don't know, but I think the old man has had something like this figured out a long time ago. I think he probably had it all mapped out with a certain police captain and they were just waiting for the right time and circumstance."

"What's their motive?" asked Sam.

"Revenge," said Jack. "They both lost children or grandchildren who O.D.ed on Don Diego's drugs."

"Come on," said Jack. "I'll give you a ride back to your hotel."

"What's your interest in Maria?" Jack asked abruptly.

"I think I'm in love," said Sam.

"Don't B.S. me," said Jack. "I've known her and her

family for a long time. They are good people and I don't want to see her hurt."

"How about you start looking for a new secretary and mind your own business."

Sam gave that last remark a few seconds to sink in and then asked, "Do you want a check to hold until Monday? I can probably get the cash then."

"A check will be fine," said Jack. "I can have my banker check it out Monday morning."

Maria picked Sam up at the hotel and announced they were going to stop by her parents' house, so that her parents could meet him. "They still think they must approve all my dates," said Maria.

Maria's mother was in a wheelchair, but was quick to tell Sam, "I don't spend my whole life in this chair. I can still stand and take a few steps." Maria's father insisted that Sam have a glass of "his wine". "I get it straight from the grower and bottle it myself. You can call me Henry, if you like, my name is Enrique which is the same as Henry in English. How did you get to be a master sergeant at such a young age?"

"At the right place at the right time, I guess," said Sam.

After a few minutes, Maria hustled Sam out saying that they had to leave. When they got outside, Maria said, "Dad would talk all night if you let him. I knew he would like you."

Dinner was delicious and Maria remarked that Sam handled the Mexican spices very well.

"I learned that in nursery school in El Paso. By the time I started kindergarten in Mississippi, I could eat very hot Mexican food and speak Spanish pretty well."

When they arrived back at the Hilton, Maria pulled

into an empty parking spot and said, "We have to talk, Sam. Jack told me what you said about looking for someone to take my place. I'm afraid, Sam, and I don't want to get too serious about you until you get through this thing against Don Diego. He is a very dangerous man. When this is all over with, I think that I would very much like to know you better. I haven't felt this way about any man in a long time."

"Oh, I'm sorry, Maria. I didn't mean to leave you with the impression that I wanted to get married. Actually it was Alabama I was thinking of. The only way he's going with me is if you come along also. I didn't mean for you to get the wrong impression."

Sam thought that Maria's dark eyes got darker. She leaned over and grabbed his shirt collar with both hands and said, "You are impossible. It's no wonder that your dog doesn't like you, but I still do. You get one kiss, Sam and nothing else until you are finished with this project." After the kiss, she pushed him toward the door, but the kiss told Sam all he needed to know.

On Sunday morning the three guys picked up a Sunday paper and started looking through the used cars for sale section. There were a few cars available that fit the description. Sam insisted that they buy a car rather than let Sparky steal one. "I don't want one of us to be thrown in jail trying to save a couple thousand bucks or whatever," said Sam.

Harold thought the prices were high for cars that were twelve or fourteen years old, with more than 200 thousand miles on them.

"They use those "jungle cruisers" for rallies," Sparky explained. "They drive them through creeks, over rocks, and up sand dunes. Most of those rally guys have big mechanical aptitudes and low I.Q.s."

They found one advertised for $1400. "Body rough, but runs okay. Can be seen at Indian River Center parking lot, N.W. corner."

"It's a shopping center over northeast," said Sparky. "Let's go have a look."

"We can take the rental car," said Sam.

"Okay," said Sparky "but I need to get some tools out of my car."

They found the shopping center and the car was where it should be.

"Don't park too close," said Sparky. He walked up to the vehicle, took a flat blade out of his tool bag and unlocked the driver's side door. He then popped the hood, got out, opened the hood and checked a few things. He got back into the car and said, "I'll check it out. If the owner shows up, tell him I'll be right back."

Sparky returned in just a few minutes and said, "It should be okay. Give me $1200. I'll leave it on the floor mat and we'll call the man." Sparky punched in the phone number of the owner and when the man on the other end answered, said "I will buy your car for $1200."

"Do you want to drive it first?" asked the owner.

"I already did," said Sparky. "Leave the key and the signed title on the floorboard, take the money and run. Don't try to remember this phone number that's calling you. Curiosity killed the cat."

"Let's move over a few cars and watch," said Sparky. About ten minutes later a car drove up beside the rally vehicle. The driver got out, looked all around and unlocked the vehicle. He removed something off the floor of the vehicle and put it in his front pocket. He then removed an envelope from his rear pocket, laid it on the floorboard, got back in his car and left.

"Looks like we bought ourselves a "jungle cruiser," said Sparky. "I'll drive it back to the hotel but you guys better follow close behind me."

As they followed Sparky back to the Hilton, Sam said to Harold, "Now that was neatly done. There were no witnesses to that transaction. That may give you a clue as to how Sparky earned his money when he was a young man."

"Yes," said Harold, "but he didn't keep the cars, he only kept the radios and tape players, which he sold to his friends and friends of his friends."

When they got back to the hotel, Sparky parked the new purchase and waved at the other two, signaling he wanted to talk. "Lopez called and he should be here in a few minutes. He said he got everything and saved you some money. He also said he wants a beer, a very cold beer. You don't need to worry, he only drinks one. You want something, Captain?"

"A Coke please," said Harold.

"One beer," said Sam. "Bring it up to my room and we'll talk."

Harold, Lopez and Sparky all trooped into Sam's room at the same time. "We still need to find the right auto dealer's name to go on the back of the vehicle," said Sam.

"Lopez and I will pick one up tonight," said Sparky. "There will be twenty thousand vehicles at the soccer game. We will sneak out halfway through the game and find one. No problem."

"That seems like a lot of trouble to go to," said Sam.

"Who you talking to man? Us Latinos like soccer!"

Sam turned to Lopez. "Your shopping trip go okay?"

"I saved you a lot of money on the sniper's rifle. The other stuff was about what I expected. I test fired the rifle in a shooting range. It works fine and I got twenty rounds of high velocity ammo. I didn't have time to check out the scope but it was in its original case. You will need to check it out at about five hundred yards. If your target is further away than five hundred yards, you adjust it one click for each additional one hundred yards."

Sam broke in, "Harold will be the shooter if there is one. I really need you, Lopez, to go with him to Jackson Hole, if you can. I would like for both of you to leave in the morning in this same van, if that's possible."

"No problem," said Lopez. "I told my boss I might take a few days vacation. It's cool."

"Sparky and I will stay here until Wednesday a.m. and then fly up there. You two will maybe have a plan of attack by then."

Harold spoke up and asked if there were any new messages from Prince Valiant.

"I'll get my computer and check," said Sparky. "If there is no message, Lopez and I are going to score some soccer tickets before the game starts. We will see you tomorrow."

A few minutes later Sparky called Sam and said, "There was one message from Prince Valiant. The message was, 'Beware of tracks left in the snow.' I acknowledged the message and signed it Oakie One."

Chapter 8

If there was one word that could describe Benjamin Bradford III, it would be "gracious." "Call me Bennie," he said. "I probably have the room too cool for you. What can I get you to drink? I can't tell you how grateful I am for the help you are giving Ellen in trying to locate Hannah Lea. I understand you paid for the charter plane and loaned Ellen money for the incident that Jack Downs pulled off. I will reimburse you for that and any other of your expenses."

"No hurry," said Sam, "I've contracted for another operation. This next one is going to cost $50 thousand. I'll tell you later about it or maybe Jack can tell you. Right now cash seems to be our only asset. In Afghanistan, the Captain (pointing at Harold) could get choppers, drones, or a battalion of infantry if he needed it. Here in L.A., we don't know the terrain, the enemy, or where the hostage is being held or even by whom for sure. The only saving grace is that our prime suspect deserves whatever happens to him even if he is not the guilty party."

"Have you heard any more from Prince Valiant?"

asked Bennie.

"Just that there is a nurse on duty in Jackson Hole and a warning to cover our tracks."

"That could be very significant. Why would they need a nurse for a caretaker crew? If anyone of the staff was ill or injured, they would go to a local doctor or clinic, right?"

"Right," said Sam.

"Sam," said Bennie, "I want you to know that Hannah means almost as much to me as she does to Ellen. I haven't been able to spend as much time with her as I wanted to, but we've managed to see each other a lot over the years. We've shown up at the same ski lodges, tennis tournaments, and other places at the same time. My wife, Brenda, is very fond of Hannah also. Hannah, by the way, shares my love for trout fishing and we plan fishing trips to different trout streams around the country. In fact, we both have reservations at a nice spot in Oregon late next month. She is a very strong young woman and is going to be a very fine attorney. I'm not sure what firm she will join as she has several offers. My intention is to hire her away in a few years for my firm."

"We will do our very best to help get her back safely," said Sam. "There is one favor I would like to ask of you, if it's not too much trouble. There was a young man who tried to rob a convenience store in Atlanta, Saturday before last. I helped disarm him but I'd like to see him have a qualified attorney to represent him. I'll be glad to pay the legal fee if there is someone available in your office to defend him."

Bennie wrote down the name of the C-store, the date, and said "I will handle it. My firm will have a qualified defense attorney handle the case pro bono. We do a considerable amount of pro bono work. If the young man is an addict, we might be able to get the sentence suspended, if he agrees to go into a drug treatment program. Would you be willing to contribute to a treatment program?"

"Yes," said Sam.

"I'll see what can be done," said Bennie.

Sam and Harold went back to their own rooms. Harold said he was going to call room service and call Amanda.

"I'm looking forward to meeting Amanda," said Sam. "I hope she doesn't hate me too much for stealing you away."

"It won't be you who gets the blame," said Harold. "I'm going to call Lopez early in the morning and get started to Wyoming. Call me if you have any last minute instructions."

"There was another message from Prince Valiant saying that we should cover our tracks well in Jackson Hole. When you check with a realtor about expensive homes, you have a legitimate reason to be there. Lopez doesn't have an excuse to be there and maybe he should stay in a nearby town rather than Jackson Hole. If you need to rent a garage or other building that probably should also be done in a nearby town."

Sam decided he would also call room service for dinner. There was very little that he could do during the next forty-eight hours before the Tuesday night operation. Maria had told him she wouldn't see him again until "this thing with Don Diego was over with." However, she didn't say that he couldn't call her. He first tried her home number. Maria's mom answered and said that Maria was at church, but should be home soon. Sam left the hotel number and his room number.

What if she doesn't call? Maybe she got really angry about that comment that I just needed her to take care of my dog. That was a really stupid remark.

The longer Sam waited, the more he became persuaded that she would never talk to him again. It seemed like several hours but actually it was only about thirty-five minutes later when the phone rang.

"This is Sam," he said with his fingers crossed.

"I'm glad you called me, Sam, I thought about calling you."

"I wanted to apologize for the stupid remark I made about needing you to take care of my ungrateful dog."

"Well, I wanted to tell you that I'm sorry I said I didn't want to see you again until your kidnapping problem is over with. That was selfish of me."

"Well, I was going to offer to make beef stroganoff for you and your parents tomorrow night, if that would be okay. Maybe Henry could help me and us guys could cook for you and your mom."

"Did Dad say you could call him Henry?"

"Yes, he did."

"Well then, I guess he approves of you. Do you remember how to get to our house?"

"I memorized every turn."

"Okay, call me if you get lost. Bye"

Actually Sam had not memorized every turn, but he had a GPS and knew her address. He watched a news channel for a while and was preparing to go to bed when his phone rang again. It was Bennie wanting to know if Sam could meet him for breakfast. "6:30 in the dining room?"

"Sure, I'll be there."

Bennie wanted to ask about the conversation that Sam and Harold had with Jones. "Does the CIA really think that a cabal of Russia, Venezuela, Iran and Mexico could actually bring down the U.S.?"

"I don't know," said Sam. "I think he is more concerned with the amount of debt the U.S. is creating and the chance that the U.S. economy will implode by itself if the present economic policies are pursued for another four years."

"He may be correct there," said Bennie. "There is one other thing I wanted to ask you about. Jones said something about the $1.4 trillion that the ex U.S. treasurer, ex governor of an Eastern U.S. state, and ex hedge fund manager somehow managed to lose. If anyone could track down that money, it would be Charlie Wong. Did Ellen tell you about her boyfriend?"

"She just said that Charlie Wong knows as much about investments as anyone in the country."

"That's true. He also knows how funds are transferred around a dozen different banks, if you want to hide the money. Now Ellen wouldn't tell you this but Charlie's nickname is 'Long Dong', not that that has anything to do with him personally, but has to do with the fact that 'Long Dong' Wong knows what's going on throughout the world. If some obscure, out of the way bank should come up with an increase in deposits of that amount Charlie Wong might be able to find out where it came from."

"That is way above my pay grade," said Sam, "but if the man really stole that money, I would like to see him pay for it. I would also like to see the 'mad Hungarian billionaire' totally out of U.S. politics."

"I'll call Charlie Wong," said Bennie.

Sam walked out into the parking lot and punched the number for Harold's phone. "You still here?" asked Sam.

"Getting ready to leave."

"I need a voided check from you before you go," said Sam.

"I'm around back with Sparky and Lopez," said Harold.

Sam walked around to the back of the hotel parking lot. Sparky's car was parked beside the rental van and the three guys were discussing something in very low tones.

"It's the timer and the detonator for the explosive pack," said Harold.

"Let me see," said Sam. "I'm familiar with that timer. Set the minutes and hours to zero, push the second setting all the way to thirty and then bring it back very, very carefully to the delay you want it set for, push the red button and run like hell!"

"Right," said Lopez.

"Does the rally vehicle have a hand throttle?" asked Sam.

"Yes," said Sparky, "and that simplifies the operation a lot. I have a six-foot long, one inch by four inch board with a notch cut out to hold the clutch pedal down. One person will hold the clutch down. The other person will make sure the transmission is set in low range and the shift lever is in first gear. Turn the steering wheel to the direction you want the vehicle to go in and secure it firmly. Tie the rope around one side of the steering wheel, run the other end of the rope around the driver's seat frame two or three tight loops and then tie it securely to the other side of the steering wheel. You probably don't want the vehicle to crash into the front door of the house. When everything is ready, start the engine, hold the clutch down with the one by four, and make sure you are clear and won't get tangled up with each other. Pull the throttle out, push the red button on the timer, and jerk the one by four away from the clutch as fast as you can. The driver's door is going to slam shut very quickly and you want the one by four to be clear, then run!"

Sam called the Jackson Federal Bank and arranged to have $20 thousand transferred to Harold's bank account. He then called Sparky and asked him to check the personals from the L.A. Times. A few minutes later Sparky called back and said there was no news.

Sam sat in the recliner chair in his room, leaned back and let his mind wander. There was very little he could do until after Tuesday night and nothing bothered him more than having to wait helplessly, feeling totally out of control. He called Sparky again, "Are you ready to deliver the vehicle to the service station?"

"Anytime you say."

"Meet you out back in ten minutes, said Sam.

"It's about a twenty minute ride," said Sparky. "I know where it is. If you lose me, you can put the address in your GPS."

A grandfatherly type gentleman walked out of the service station, smiled at Sam and said, "We will take care of it and drop it off at this address tomorrow night. Leave the packet and the detonator with me. We are going to attach it to the front of the firewall and run some wires through to attach to the timer. Jack Downs is going to give you a ride tomorrow night to where this vehicle will be parked. An off duty police car will be there to take you out of the area."

"How many people are in on this?" asked Sam.

"They all have tight lips, so it really doesn't matter, does it?"

"No, it doesn't," said Sam, "Thanks."

Driving back to the hotel Sam asked Sparky if there were two-way communication devices that were secure for two parties to communicate with.

"How far apart do you want to talk?" asked Sparky.

"Just a few miles."

"Sure, the Computer Shack has them for twenty bucks."

"Can you pick us up two sets?"

Sam gave Sparky an envelope. "There's three thousand dollars in it for your first three days pay. Hang loose until I need you. We will either fly out late tomorrow night or early Wednesday morning."

It seemed like an eternity went by for Sam to kill two hours and call Ellen.

"Nothing is new here, Sam. The FBI claims they've interviewed over a hundred people in the area, practically everyone she's had contact with during her three years in law school. They talked to some people with the Miss Arizona contest and even sent some agents to Vanderbilt University, where she got her undergraduate degree. They've reduced the number of agents who are active on the case and tomorrow will be their last day to hold a briefing until something new turns up. The only positive thing I can tell you is that last night I dreamed that Hannah and I were fishing together."

"Fishing?" asked Sam.

"Yes, fly fishing," said Ellen, "and that's something

that I know absolutely nothing about."

"That could be a very good sign," said Sam. But he didn't elaborate. He suspected that could be a positive message from God and thought to himself, why would someone who hardly knew that fly fishing existed dream about it? "Harold and Lopez left this morning for Wyoming. Sparky and I will fly there either late tomorrow night or early Wednesday morning. We can send the plane for you tomorrow afternoon, if you like."

"Not necessary," said Ellen. "Bennie says he'll be done with the legal work in L.A. tomorrow and he is flying back here. We are both going to stay here through Wednesday and stay in touch with the FBI."

"Stay strong, Ellen. You are not the only one praying for Hannah Lea."

Sam was too antsy to wait any longer. He took a shower, changed clothes and left for Jack Downs' office to check on Alabama. He didn't see Jack but Maria was at her desk, talking on the phone. She held up one finger and continued talking for a few seconds. "I need to talk to you about my ungrateful dog," said Sam. "We will fly out either late tomorrow or very early Wednesday. I can leave him with the pilots tomorrow and find a kennel for him in Jackson Hole."

"You can leave him with me. I'll take him home with me tonight. My parents like dogs and he can stay in the back yard."

"Are you sure your parents don't mind?"

"Henry likes dogs."

"You still don't believe your dad told me I could call him Henry?"

"Sure, I believe you, I just don't understand it. Someday I'll tell you why. But it's not important and

I'm glad you guys get along."

"I'm going grocery shopping," said Sam. "I wrote down all of the ingredients. I'm a little fuzzy on the order of things but it will come back to me."

"Buy some food for Alabama, he's almost out. Get this brand," she said as she wrote the name down on a piece of paper.

The evening went very well. Sam finally remembered the right sequence for making the dish. Henry cut up the steak and browned it while Sam was peeling mushrooms. They got all of the ingredients into the skillet except the mushrooms and noodles. The noodles would cook in beef broth and go into the skillet last. The mushrooms would go in just a few minutes ahead of the noodles.

Sam thought it was as good as he had ever made and appreciated the compliments. He excused himself at a fairly early hour. Maria said she would walk him out to his car. Henry made a remark about Sam needing protection and laughed. Sam shook hands with both of Maria's parents and said he hoped to see them again soon.

"Take care of yourself and call me every night," said Maria. "Can you remember that?" This time Sam got two very nice kisses and a final hug.

"I'll remember."

Chapter 9

Harold Brown and Ismael Lopez stopped for gas and coffee at an Interstate service center and Harold surrendered the keys to Ismael. When they got back on the road he called Amanda, wondering what new name she might have for him. In the last several months she had gone through "Soldier Boy", "Lover Boy", "School Boy", "Spy Master" when he was hired by the CIA, and he expected a new one any day now.

Amanda did not disappoint him. "What are you up to now, Sir Galahad?"

"I'm still trying to save the same damsel in distress," Harold answered. "Senor Lopez and I are heading for Jackson Hole and I wondered if you knew anything about the place."

"Yeah, we used to ski there and my ex considered buying a house there but they were too expensive, even for him."

"Can you remember the name of a real estate company or agent that specializes in high dollar homes?"

"Yes, there was this one lady, if I could think of her name. Rita, that's it, Rita Rosewood Real Estate. As I recall, she was a chain smoker, talked constantly, but seemed to know her business. Maybe if you could get her in an airplane and keep the no smoking light turned on, she might not smell like a cigarette!"

"Well actually, I hadn't planned on kissing her. What I had in mind was strictly business. I should be home by Sunday or Monday at the latest and you can catch me up on the kissing thing."

"Don't hesitate too long or I will be addressing you as my former 'Lover Boy'."

"Yes, Ma'am, I love you very much."

As they drove down the road, Harold leaned back in his seat and reflected on his military career. It started at Oklahoma State University. When he first arrived at the University as a freshman, he tested out thirty-two hours in math, science, physics and literature. This made him a sophomore on his first day in school. The only exception was that he was required to take freshman ROTC. As it turned out he actually enjoyed the military training, signed up for the advanced ROTC and four years later, he left Oklahoma State with a masters degree in Ag Economics and was commissioned a second lieutenant in the U.S. Army. Four years later, he was wearing the captain's "railroad tracks" silver bars and had completed every officer's leadership course that his rank permitted, including ranger training.

Harold had served in both Iraq and Afghanistan and was a few weeks away from rotating back stateside as a Major when his army career came to a sudden end.

That hurt. It hurt more than the loss of his left hand. His commanding officer, Colonel Smith, had told him, "You have a place reserved in the war college course at Carlyle, Pennsylvania. You will probably be an aide de camp for a Colonel or a General and eventually you will be attending the General and Command school in Leavenworth, Kansas.

Harold's team had been selected to destroy an enemy bomb factory that was producing road side bombs and suicide bomber packs in a town about one hundred kilometers from his base. Top brass had decided to take out the bomb factory with a surgically placed explosive rather than an air strike. They did not want the bad publicity that would arise if Afghan civilians were killed. The Taliban had started producing bombs in what had been a school for young boys.

The six man force was choppered in about eight kilometers from the town. The chopper would then back off a safe distance and watch for the explosion or radio communications and then dash back in to within a few hundred yards for the pickup.

The force took up a position behind a retaining wall, with the targeted school building to their left and a Mosque to their right. The six man force consisted of First Lieutenant Armenio, Staff Sergeant Payne, Lopez was next with two packets of high explosives, then Sparky and Sam immediately to the Captain's left. Harold spoke in low tones saying, "Set the timer for forty-five seconds. Payne and Sparky cover the front of the school. Sam will secure the front of the Mosque." At that instant the Captain saw the figure emerge from the shadows beside the church and saw the grenade coming toward him. The Captain screamed, "Down, down, grenade" as he stood up and knocked the grenade down on the other side of the retaining wall. He dived for cover and almost made it. His outstretched left hand was the only part of his body still above the retaining wall when the grenade exploded. There was very little left of his left hand.

"You are in charge, Armenio! Get it done and get us out of here!"

The Captain pulled a rubber tube out of his belt and held one end in his mouth and stretched the tube around his arm, two loops as tight as he could and tied the tube off. The hand was still gushing blood but slower now. He watched as Lieutenant Armenio ran out between the school and the Mosque. The Lieutenant checked in the direction of where Sam was. He apparently saw something in front of him and fired off a burst from his machine gun. He then turned toward the front of the school, and saw Lopez running back making a winding motion with his arm over his head, indicating the timer on the explosives was winding down.

Armenio saw that Payne, Lopez and Sparky were all running towards the back of the Mosque and that Sam was running towards Captain Brown.

"Don't get too close to the Mosque," Armenio shouted, "there may be a lot of debris falling down!"

Sam got his right arm around Harold's waist and pulled Harold's left arm around his own waist and squeezed as hard as he could to stop the flow of blood. Armenio got on the Captain's right side, put the Captain's right arm around his neck, reached behind the Captain and grasped his belt so that he and Sam were practically carrying the Captain. Captain Brown tried to keep his feet moving, but did not remember being hauled aboard the chopper.

Captain Brown would find out later that the army surgeons in Afghanistan did a fine job of removing what was left of his left hand and making a smooth stub where his wrist joint had been.

The majors, colonels, and generals who came to visit all wished him well. He was also told that he had been recommended to receive a Silver Star for endangering his own life by standing up to knock down the grenade.

Brown's immediate commanding officer, Colonel Smith, told him "We should have sent in a drone. There must have been a ton of bomb explosives in that school building. Everything around the school, except the Mosque, was flattened."

"No one knew that," said Harold. "The right decision was made."

Harold continued, "You know Armenio did a heck of a job taking over. He called it perfectly and made sure everyone was accounted for. His warning that debris would be raining down from the back of the Mosque was brilliant. No one else thought of that."

"Sergeant Dallas said the same thing. Lieutenant Armenio will be rewarded for his leadership."

"Is Armenio taking over my job?" asked Brown.

"No," said the Colonel. "But he is getting his captain's bars and is heading back to the States for ranger training."

"He's earned it," said Brown.

Captain Brown's stay at Walter Reed U.S. Army Hospital was more boring than anything. No further surgery was required on his arm, no other problems were observed and he was mainly killing time until his stub healed sufficiently to get fitted with a prosthetic device.

Wilbur and Judy Brown flew in shortly after he arrived at Walter Reed. They stayed an entire week in the Washington, D.C. area. They brought him books, some new civilian clothes and spent hours with him. They told him that Amanda Stevens had been at their church the previous Sunday and had asked about him. Amanda had been his tutor in fifth grade and had got him completely turned around in his understanding of math.

"Amanda is married, isn't she?" asked Harold.

"Not anymore," Judy said. "She is divorced and is back at Oklahoma University and working on a PhD degree in mathematics.

Harold had liked Amanda a lot, even though they never actually dated, but had wound up together on two occasions. Once during a hay ride when Amanda's date didn't show up and later at the back of the school bus when they were coming home from a debating contest in another town. "If I had known you could kiss like that, I would have asked you for a date," said Harold.

"Why would I go out with you?" Amanda asked. "You are too young, too short and too stupid." But she had kissed him again.

When Judy excused herself to go find a "Ladies", Wilbur said, "Listen up boy, I'm sorry as hell about your hand, but I'm tickled to death about your being out of the army. As soon as you get your new hand or whatever you get, then get yourself back to Oklahoma. We intend to sell you the farm at a price you can afford. There's a good amount of natural gas income from it now, plus the farm income. We want to get that done right away, so that the farm will stay in the family."

"Do you think your old grandpa would approve of that?" asked Harold.

"The old bastard would be very proud," said Wilbur.

"I would really love that," said Harold, "and someday I want to move there, tend some cattle, catch some fish and gig some frogs, if there's still some in the bay, but first I'm going back to Oklahoma State and do more research in agricultural economics. If I get accepted, I intend to work on a PhD degree."

"That's not a problem," said Wilbur.

The next week Harold was transferred to the "hand unit" in a nearby rehab clinic that provided recovering veterans with prosthetic devices.

"You can have your choice," said a technician, "either an artificial hand that will open and close or you can have a pair of forceps that will give you better control and are faster to learn how to use."

"Can I change later?" asked Harold.

"Of course," said the technician, "you are covered for life. You can get a replacement every five years or less if there is a problem."

"Let's go with the forceps," said Harold.

On Thursday, Amanda Stevens showed up at the rehab center. "You left Walter Reed without leaving a change of address but I found you anyhow."

"I'm glad you found me. You look nice."

"I asked if I could take you to lunch and they said I could have you until three o'clock this afternoon. They also said I could have you this weekend."

"What did you have in mind for the weekend?"

"I didn't decide. Maybe the Chesapeake, the Outer Banks, Delaware, whatever. Let's go get some lunch now and we can decide later."

Harold was glad he had showered and shaved earlier in the morning. "Do I need to change clothes?"

"You are fine, let's go."

A few minutes later, Amanda left the Interstate and

two minutes after that, pulled into the basement parking lot of a nice hotel. "We're up on the fourteenth floor, Soldier Boy. You know that's actually the thirteenth floor, since hotels go directly from twelve to fourteen."

"I'm not worried about the number thirteen."

"But you are worried about me."

"No, I know you are a fine, gentle woman."

"That's a laugh, I forgot that you were an Eagle Scout."

Amanda's room was spacious with a stunning view of several of Washington, D.C.'s more famous monuments. There was a bottle of white wine and a bucket of ice. "I'll open that for us. It might take you a while."

They sat at a table in a kitchenette area, clinked glasses and Amanda asked what his plans were.

"I'm going to spend a few days at home. Wilbur and Judy want to sell me the farm. I might do some fishing if I can find a nice lady to bait my hook for me. Are you interested?"

"That's one proposition I've never been offered before. Maybe."

Harold laughed and said, "Actually, I want to do more research in
Ag Econ. If I can qualify to get into a doctorate program, that's what I intend to do."

"You know that you can do that in a joint program between Oklahoma State and Oklahoma University. OSU will approve any PhD courses in economics or math that you take at O.U."

"If I could find a math tutor in Oak City, that might work."

"I'll ask around. Do you want a bit more wine before we order lunch?"

"No"

"What do you want?"

"I want to know how to undo a lady's buttons with only one hand."

Amanda pulled her chair around by his chair, sat down and kissed him, very slowly, several times. "It's very simple, Soldier Boy. You just ask the lady to help you."

After lunch they resumed talking about Harold's educational ambitions. "You know that your master's thesis got a lot of attention," Amanda said.

"From whom?"

"From a friend of your old advisor at OSU. Your advisor's friend is very high up here in Washington. Your old advisor, Dr. Harkin, told me that."

"Dr. Harkin is still at OSU?"

"He's head of the Ag Econ Department."

"How did you meet him?"

"He was at a party at my advisor's house. When I told him what town I was from, he asked if I knew you."

"So you told him you taught me all the math I would ever need."

"Of course. Let's get you back to the body parts factory."

They walked back into the clinic and Amanda said, "I'll wait for you here."

"What are you waiting for?"

"I'm waiting for them to measure you up. After they get you measured, they won't need you until next Monday."

"Are you absolutely sure?"

"Yes, I'll wait for you."

Their weekend was absolutely glorious. The sights, the food, the love making and the catching up. It had been over twelve years since they had graduated from high school.

Amanda talked about her failed marriage, the excitement of the trips, the boating in Florida and the Bahamas. Her ex was a very young bank president and principle owner and had been very successful at growing an already successful bank. She had met him at a seminar where he spoke and the banker had been impressed with both her beauty and her brains.

They had eight years together before she began to suspect that he might have someone else in his life. She hired a detective and got ten times more evidence than she needed. She showed him copies of the evidence. He said she could have the house, the car, and $100 thousand. She countered with $5 million and threatened to keep dribbling out juicy tidbits, including his trysts with a couple of prominent married women. They settled for $2.5 million, the house, and two cars, one of which was an eighty thousand dollar sports car. She really did not care much for the sports car, it was more punishment than anything else.

Harold talked about his four years at Oklahoma State University, the ROTC program and the fact that he sincerely enjoyed the military experience. He told her a little bit about his ranger training and Amanda asked if he actually ate snakes.

"No," said Harold. "But I ate some other things you don't want to hear about."

As they were getting ready to drive back to the "body parts factory", Amanda said, "We need to talk seriously about the future."

"Okay," said Harold. "Where are we escaping to next weekend?"

"Don't be cute, Soldier Boy. I didn't come here just for a weekend. I'm talking about the rest of our lives."

Harold answered, "I accept your offer of a lifetime employment contract. How much will my salary be?"

"Asshole!" Amanda said. "You know what I mean."

"I know," said Harold, "and I couldn't be happier about having you for my wife. I'm serious."

"I know you love action, hunting, fishing and skiing when you learn how to hold a ski pole. The one thing I won't put up with is other women."

"And I won't put up with you having other men. That works both ways."

Harold forced himself to bring his mind back to the present even though he very much preferred to think about Amanda. He found the number for the Rosewood Realty firm and was surprised when Rita herself answered the phone. Harold explained that he was doing some advance scouting for a good friend who was looking for a nice home in Jackson Hole.

"What price range is your friend thinking about?" asked Ms. Rosewood.

"Probably in the mid single digits."

"You mean single digit millions, of course."

"Well, of course," said Harold. "Is there a helicopter service available? I would like to get a good overview with an aerial photo, if possible before I recommend anything to my friend."

"Helicopter service is available but I don't pop for that service for someone I haven't done business with before. You pay for the 'bird' and if you buy something, I will reimburse you from my commission. Fair enough?"

"Sounds very fair. Do you have some time available tomorrow afternoon?"

"I can schedule a helicopter for one o'clock tomorrow. Stop by my office tomorrow morning and leave a deposit for the helicopter." Rita gave Harold the address of her office and hung up.

Harold checked his map and chose a town about twenty miles from Jackson Hole and told Lopez they would try to get a room there. "Sam and Sparky will be in town Wednesday morning and Sparky can get a room at the same hotel you are staying at. Sam and I have an excuse to be in Jackson Hole, as we are looking for a very nice house to buy. You and Sparky don't have an excuse to be there and whatever preparations we have to make need to be done several miles away from Jackson Hole."

"That makes sense," said Lopez. "I don't want to leave any footprints behind."

They found a nice motel about twenty miles west of Jackson Hole and stopped for the night. Harold asked if internet service was available and was assured that it was. He checked for messages from Prince Valiant and there were none.

Chapter 10

Don Diego never felt more optimistic as he left early Tuesday morning for San Francisco. He would meet first with the Bay Area Director of Operations for the Latin Pizzaz Corporation. The two would then meet with the CEO of the largest department store chain in the U.S. The purpose was to get a "hand shake agreement" for a joint venture that would allow Latin Pizzaz to establish retail counters in select stores of the national retail chain. If the market test worked successfully, the two corporations would expand the concept nationally.

That meeting did go very well and a target date was set to implement a market test at three Bay Area department stores. Don Diego then attended a Bay Area Progressive Political Party meeting and pledged support for the candidates running for office in the coming elections. He stayed for cocktails, had his picture taken with the Congresswoman who represented the central part of San Francisco and arranged to have dinner with a wealthy influential lady whom he had long admired. The dinner at her apartment went very well, as they discussed the Bay Area business, political, and social situations. When it was time for him to leave, she had first given him her cheek to kiss and then had surprised him with a light kiss on his lips. As she let him out the door, she said, "Let me know when you will be in town next time and maybe we can spend more time together."

Don Diego's chauffeur dropped him at his San Francisco apartment and the caretaker couple greeted him warmly and asked if he would like something to eat or drink.

"A small glass of sherry, please." Overall he had had a very successful day. He made a note in his calendar to schedule another trip to San Francisco and to be sure to check and make sure that the nice socialite lady would be available. It would be a date - sort of.

He went to sleep anticipating pleasant dreams, but was awakened two hours later by his apartment caretaker.

"Paul Hastings is on the phone, sir, and he says it's very urgent."

"What's going on, Paul? Snapped Don Diego.

"All hell has broken loose at the main house here," was the answer. "Someone crashed an old jungle cruiser through the guard station gate and it blew up about forty feet from the front doors. I wasn't here but Jake said that several police cars arrived almost immediately. Several cops broke in and said they were required to search every room for injured persons. They 'found' about six ounces of cocaine, which of course, they had planted themselves."

"Are you sure it was a setup?"

"Absolutely, Diego. I had the entire staff tested for

drug use last month. They all know they can't use and they can't deal. They know what the penalty is if they try."

"See what you can find out and pick me up at the airport. I'll call you when we're wheels up."

Don Diego went back to bed, but slept very little. He finally got out of bed at six o'clock, called his chief pilot and told him to prepare for takeoff as soon as possible.

It was almost nine o'clock by the time they arrived back at LAX and Diego was met by Paul Hastings. They drove through what once had been massive steel gates to the remains of the jungle cruiser. From the windshield forward, the vehicle had vanished. The top was lifted grotesquely skyward and the interior had burned out. For some strange reason, the gas tank had not exploded. The back lift gate was still intact and the chrome name of the auto dealership was still in place. "You don't suppose that idiot in Northeast L.A. is behind this, do you?"

"He's too smart to try something like this," said Paul. "More than likely it was some rogue cops."

"I pay the cops and the politicians plenty," said Don Diego. "They have no reason to do this."

Paul Hastings' phone rang and he listened for a few seconds and then said, "You tell him. I'm not giving him any more bad news". He handed his phone to Don Diego.

It was the Chief Corporate Counsel of the Latin Pizzaz Corporation saying that "we are being sued by a group of small competitors for $50 million and treble damages for restraint of trade and monopolistic practices. I signed for receipt of the lawsuit on your behalf."

Don Diego did not answer. He threw Paul's telephone down to the ground, stamped on it repeatedly and was yelling curses at the top of his lungs in at least two different languages. He finally took a deep breath and said to Hastings, "Let's go to the office, Paul."

They drove out onto the Interstate and immediately came to a halt in a massive traffic jam. Don Diego wondered what else could go wrong. "You think Tony Raymond did this?" asked Don Diego.

"Why would he? He runs a good organization and hasn't had a shipment lost in over three years. His record on losing dealers to the cops is way above average."

"He's also one of only two distributors who know the system well enough to take over the whole operation."

"Well, yes, because he worked as a key man and a troubleshooter directly for you."

"Look," said Don Diego. "I want you to send him a message. Blow up something of his or shoot one of his guys in the leg, then set up a meeting with him and we'll talk."

"I'll go see him as soon as I drop you off and pick up a new cell phone. You maybe should consider one thing, the fire in the store, this attack on your house, and now this lawsuit; all of that started since I grabbed that girl off the street last week."

"You don't really think they're connected, do you Paul? That girl is the daughter of a single mom according to the article in the Phoenix paper."

"Maybe so, but someone showed the girl how to fight. She elbowed the fat nurse behind the ear, kneed her in the crotch and head butted her in the nose."

"When did this happen?"

"About the second day she was there in Jackson Hole. One of the guards had to help restrain her."

"Well, I'm glad you told me. That will make it more interesting, won't it?" said Don Diego, as he rubbed his hands together.

Paul Hastings walked into the owner's outer office of the auto dealership in Northeast L.A. and told the secretary that it was urgent. The secretary said, "Let me check for you, Mr. Hastings." A minute later she said, "Go on in."

"Let's go for a walk," Paul told Tony Raymond.

They walked outside and Raymond asked, "What's going on?"

"The Don thinks you might have been behind the incident at his big house last night."

"Tell the Don, number one, I'm not pissed at him, number two, I don't have designs on his empire and number three, whoever did that was either an idiot or an amateur or both, if they thought they were going to eliminate the Don. Was he even there?"

"No," said Paul.

"Did you have your radio on driving over here?"

"No again. I was breaking in a new cell phone."

"Well, L.A. Instant News is out with a story that the police found a sizable amount of cocaine when they investigated the break-in at Don Diego's house last night. The online L.A. Times has a story about it also. I think this is very serious and I'm pulling some of my dealers off the street until things cool down. You better get Don Diego out of that meeting and figure out how to handle this before it totally blows up."

Chapter 11
Day 7, Wednesday morning
Jackson Hole Municipal Airport

Harold Brown met Sam's chartered plane at nine a.m.

"Where's Lopez?" asked Sam.

"He's busy working and we'll catch up with him later," said Harold. "He and I went on a chopper ride yesterday and the rest of us will go on the same chopper this morning. It's ready to go. The real estate lady will be here shortly, so if anyone needs to use the facilities or get a cup of coffee, do it now."

"I'm okay," said Sam, as Sparky headed for the terminal building. "What's the program?"

"The real estate lady's name is Rita Rosewood and she's bringing with her aerial photos of the area that we looked at yesterday. Sam, you need to sit on the left side of the chopper and when Rita says something about the Peterson mansion, she's talking about Don Diego's house. She will also mention farmer Brown's property, which is adjacent to Don Diego's property. When we fly over Mr. Brown's farm, if you look to your left, you will get a good look at the rear of Don Diego's house."

As the chopper gained altitude, Rita began to point out the different sights and said that the main areas they would be looking at were all on a high plateau, not far from the ski area. "The view is absolutely spectacular," gushed Rita.

Sam was gracious in complimenting the properties in the first area but said he would like a bit more acreage that could accommodate a few cows and horses. Rita replied that she personally didn't have any properties with acreage in the nice areas that Sam was interested in, but she would check with some other realtors. "I would like nothing better than to sell you the Peterson property. This new owner has been such a disappointment compared to the original owner and his son who followed him. The house was built after World War II by a General Peterson, who served on Eisenhower's staff in England and took part in the D-Day landing in Normandy. Both he and his eldest son, who moved into the mansion after his parents moved to Florida, really knew how to throw a party. The entire first floor was designed for entertaining guests. You enter through those huge oak doors that are said to be four inches thick, into a ballroom with a dance floor on the left, a huge bar on the right and a cozy area to the right of that for those who don't care to dance. The rear part of the first floor consisted of a huge dining room and kitchen, capable of feeding fifty people or more. The family actually lived on the second floor with a smaller kitchen, dining room and a living area with panoramic views on all sides. The basement is a large recreation area with two pool tables, a ping pong table and a television viewing area."

"The present owner is a Spanish or Mexican Duke or

something who very seldom comes here and then for only a few days at a time. For him, it's just an escape and he never has guests. What a shame!"

When they flew around farmer Brown's property, Sam asked if she thought the farmer might like to sell some of his acreage.

"No, he won't sell you any of his land," said Rita. "But he will be glad to talk to you. He likes people and you will enjoy talking to him. I'll call him and ask if I can give you his phone number. He'll say yes. He has a working ranch and sells hay and grain to the owner of the Peterson mansion."

When they landed back at the airport and Rita left them, Harold told Sam that he had already met farmer Brown and that they were already buddies. "He was a Green Beret in Viet Nam and when I told him I went through Ranger training, we became instant friends. I told him I had a new rifle that I needed to check out before I went bear hunting in Siberia and he told me I could come over to his place this afternoon and check it out."

The next stop was a small warehouse building in an industrial area about twenty minutes from Jackson Hole. "We rented the warehouse for a month," said Harold. "And we also rented that pickup you see there to haul stuff. There doesn't seem to be a lot of activity in the area, so we should have plenty of privacy."

They entered the warehouse and were facing a huge H-1 Hummer vehicle. "It weighs about five or six tons and gets about five or six miles to the gallon. It is our entry vehicle into Don Diego's house."

Lopez walked up at this moment and entered the conversation by saying, "Okay, you swashbuckling soldiers of fortune, the plane rides are over with and the hard work begins."

"Lopez has a design that will allow us to enter the mansion through those huge four inch doors. I think his design will work but we have a lot of work to do between now and tomorrow night."

Lopez went back to his project, which was to install the telescope on the sniper's rifle and Harold asked Sam to look at the sketches that he and Lopez had prepared of the mansion's front entrance and the modifications they planned to add to the Hummer.

"Lopez had a good look at the main entrance to the house yesterday. There's a large stairway between two Greek column s up to a porch in front of the two massive doors. Rita described the steps as wide and flat. I think she meant that the risers are relative short. We estimated there were about fifteen steps up to the porch and another eight feet or so between the top step and the oak doors. This side view of the vehicle shows how an I-beam has to be placed to hit the two oak doors about half way up. The flat plate has to be attached to the beam at the proper angle, in order to hit the doors squarely. The rear of the I-beam is attached to the luggage rack on top of the vehicle but the support comes from these two channel iron struts that come from the front bumper, which is attached to the frame of the vehicle. That allows the frame to absorb most of the shock."

"As Rita said, everyone lives on the second floor, including the guards, the cook, and the old man who helps the cook and pays the bills. The exception to that is a security station at the north side service entrance to the mansion. Apparently that's the only entrance being used by everyone, including Don Diego. I've no idea whether the security station is manned full time or not. I suspect it's locked up tight, if there's no traffic or when Don Diego isn't there."

"According to farmer Brown, Don Diego takes coffee on the rear balcony every morning when he's there, even in wintertime, rain or shine, he's out there in his PJs and housecoat, sipping his coffee and peering through his binoculars at his Gelbvieh cattle. My suggestion is to nail him with the sniper's rifle and when he goes down and is discovered, everyone will converge on the balcony to see about him. As soon as that happens, we will charge in, knock the two doors in, take position and when the guards hear the noise and charge down the stairs, we'll be in position to nail them as they run down the steps. Maybe have two guys charge inside and the third one will run around and cover the side entrance."

"You will be the sniper," said Sam. "Where do you shoot from?"

"Because of the equipment sheds and barns, I'll have to shoot from the west end of farmer Brown's property to get a clear shot. The distance is about eight hundred yards. I can still do that. I bagged an elk in Montana last fall from about the same distance. My left arm is very strong because I operate the forceps by flexing my arm muscles."

Sam was studying the aerial photographs and pointed to a little lane just north of Don Diego's house that meandered off westward into the forest. "There probably was a house back there at one time. Let's check that out later and see if it's a good place to gather before the attack."

"Oh man, look here," said Sam. "There's this other road that leaves the main road here, loops around through the development here and comes back out on the main road on the other side of Don Diego's house. If we wanted to we could block off traffic for the ten minutes or so during the operation, maybe set up some temporary roadblocks on sawhorses and have Ellen and Bennie route traffic around while the operation is going on."

"That would keep Ellen out of the way," said Harold. "Otherwise she would demand a weapon also."

"Call your farmer Brown and see if you can zero in your rifle this afternoon. We need to know if that rifle can do the job.

Harold called the farmer, who said "Sure, you can come on out. You can park across the road from the west end of my property and I'll meet you there about two o'clock."

Harold and Lopez followed the farmer's instructions and met him at the designated place and entered the farmer's property through a removable "gap" in the fence.

"Let's walk up the fence here a ways," said the farmer pointing north. As they walked along the fence, the farmer pointed to Don Diego's house and said, "I haven't seen my wealthy neighbor in several weeks. When he's here, he's usually out there on his balcony, peering through his field glasses. I sometimes bring my own binoculars with me to make sure all of my cattle are where they're supposed to be." The farmer stopped and said to Lopez, "walk out there straight toward that power plant stack you see in the distance. When you see that dirt bank there ahead of you, you can plant your target there. If that bank doesn't stop the bullet, the trees behind it will."

As Lopez walked away, farmer Brown asked if Lopez had served with him in Afghanistan. "Yes, Lopez was my weapons and munitions specialist and he was very good at what he did. He never ever backed away from anything."

Lopez drove his two stakes in the ground, secured the target and backed off several yards.

Harold removed a clip from his pocket and slipped it into the gun. "Lopez said the scope is set for four hundred yards. I suppose if I hit him instead of the target, it's his own fault."

"I certainly hope not," said the farmer.

Harold found the target in the scope field, breathed in air, raised the gun up a little, let out some air and fired almost immediately. Harold handed the farmer a small set of binoculars and asked if he would read the spot. Lopez indicated that the round had hit about a foot below the bull's eye, but only a couple of inches to the left. Lopez then walked away and Harold prepared to shoot again. He adjusted the scope setting for height only and aimed a little to the right. Lopez spotted the second shot just a little under the bull's eye.

Harold waved for Lopez to come in for a talk. "How was the wind blowing out there?" asked Harold.

"From the northwest, pretty much from your left side, but no more than about five miles per hour," said Lopez.

"Okay," said Harold. "It's probably shooting three or four inches to the left. I did adjust for height and that's about right."

"Okay, try one click clockwise on the horizontal

adjustment."

"Let's try two more shots," said Harold and Lopez headed back towards the target.

Harold's next shot was indicated a bull's eye. His fourth shot received the same signal and Harold waved Lopez in. When Lopez arrived, Harold asked, "What would be the correction, if the distance was double?"

"Four clicks forward on the left adjustment knob. That would be counterclockwise."

"You're sure?"

"I'm positive!"

Farmer Brown looked at the target and said, "That's some might fine shooting."

"Thanks, I'm blessed with very good vision and good nerves. However, the credit goes to this man here," as he grabbed Lopez's shoulder. "He put this package together in just a couple of days - rifle, scope and silencer - and made it work."

Harold and Lopez returned to the rented warehouse and Lopez immediately joined Sparky in checking out the hardware that Sparky and Sam had purchased. Sam grabbed Harold and said, "I want to go back over with you and look at everything from ground level and make sure that you and I can see the whole picture together."

Sam was especially interested in the abandoned trail, as well as the road that veered off the main road, went through the development west of Don Diego's house and then rejoined the main road. They took odometer readings of each point and drove to the area where Harold would leave the pickup while he was waiting for his target to appear on the rear balcony. They drove back to the small lane and drove up the lane about two hundred yards to an area wide enough to turn around.

"We'll have Lopez and Sparky leave early enough to have the Hummer here by four o'clock on Friday morning. I want them to leave the warehouse by three o'clock with Sparky leading the way in the pickup. We need to give them one set of the radio phones, so they can communicate. Sparky will lead the way in the pickup and if there's an accident or police cars anywhere, he'll warn Lopez and either have him wait a few minutes or try to find a way around the police car. We'll back the Hummer up this road, far enough that it can't be seen from the main road. You'll drive the pickup down to where you'll shoot from and let us know when you see activity on the balcony. We'll have Ellen and Bennie put up the detour signs at that time. The Hummer will then move down toward the main road. Any time after that you can take your shot. When we hear you say, 'Target down', we'll head out as fast as possible. Assuming the oak doors get breached, Lopez and I will go through them and take a position. Sparky will move around to the north side of the house and cover the service entrance. As soon as you can get in your truck and get back on the road, come on in. We may still need your help. I sincerely hope your help won't be needed."

Chapter 12
Day 7, Late Wednesday afternoon
Corporate Headquarters of Latin Pizzaz, Inc.

Paul Hastings took the elevator to the top floor and asked his secretary if she knew where Don Diego was. She pointed toward the boardroom. "Are they still working on an answer to the lawsuit?"

"I think so, but Don Diego issued a statement earlier saying that all L.P. Corporation employees undergo regular drug testing and that he would never condone drug dealing by any employee and that slanderous speculation in that regard could result in the company suing for damages."

"Has that stopped the gossip?" asked Paul.

"No! It's still being mentioned at the top and bottom of every hour on the media news breaks."

"Tell his secretary that I'm back in my office and that I would like to see him as soon as he's free."

Don Diego stuck his head in Paul's office and said, "Have someone in security sweep my hotel suite within the next hour and I'll meet you there one hour from now." Paul called up the head of the internal security department and relayed Don Diego's request. He emphasized the "within the hour" part of the request and then finished with the words, "you can handle that within the hour?"

"Yes sir," was the answer.

Paul went back out to talk to his secretary. "I will need a plane day after tomorrow, Friday. Not a company plane but a chartered jet. I want to leave L.A. at 7 a.m. There will be five stops, each lasting about a half hour. We should be back in L.A. by six p.m. and all stops will be near the Pacific Coast with the exception of Las Vegas."

The secretary repeated the request and Paul said, "That's it and I'll see you on Monday."

Paul retrieved his Yukon from the parking garage, even though he would have preferred walking or taking a cab. Rush hour traffic caused what would have been a fifteen minute walk to be a thirty minute drive and did nothing to improve his attitude.

At Don Diego's apartment, he tagged along behind the bug sweepers who were working over the apartment. He decided that the A team was on the job and moved to the bar. He figured Don Diego would probably want a glass of wine and made sure there was both white and red available. Paul made himself a martini. He needed to slow his mind down.

Don Diego came in, saw Paul's martini and said, "Make me one of those, please." He took a sip from his drink and said, "I spent the day working with the lawyers on a preliminary answer to the lawsuit and in between, I spoke with the mayor, the newspaper, two TV stations and a couple of other organizations trying to quell the narcotics accusations. I have a full schedule tomorrow, meeting with the mayor again at breakfast and then a half dozen other meetings throughout the day and will finish with a full twenty minute interview on Channel 60 tomorrow night. After that, I'm flying to Jackson Hole. We probably won't get off the ground before 9:30 or 10 o'clock."

"What is the thrust of your defense?" asked Paul.

"It's more an attack than a defense. I'm telling everyone how important Latin Pizzaz is to the L.A. economy. We have more than a thousand employees just in the L.A. area with six stores, a major distribution warehouse and our corporate headquarters. There are a dozen cities between San Diego, Phoenix and San Francisco that could come up with $50 million in incentives, should we decide to move elsewhere. I'll also play the race card. They should think twice before they discriminate against a Mexican company. There could be a minor Mexican revolution come Election Day."

"For my part," said Paul, "I intend to visit each of our distributors during the next two days. I'm starting in North L.A. and will work my way south. I'm meeting with Thurman from San Diego tomorrow evening and he will meet with his brother who runs the Phoenix area the next day. On Friday, I'm flying to the four areas north of here and on to Las Vegas for my last stop."

"I'm going to insist on an immediate shut down of all street activities," Paul continued. "Our most experienced dealers will continue to service their wealthy high volume customers, but the street pushers are coming off the streets. We'll have our street guys get new phones with new numbers and have them work on finding out who their competitors are. After a few weeks, we'll squeal on our competitors and let the narcs enjoy a huge victory. After that, we'll be back on the streets, stronger than ever On Sunday I will meet with Ramon in Baja to keep the cartel informed.."

"Okay," said Don Diego. "Tell the guys that you and I are together on this and there's no discussion, no exceptions. Do you have any news from Jackson Hole?"

"The girl is still fighting all the way, even though she has diarrhea and is very weak."

Paul ate part of his dinner and excused himself to plan his two day visits to the distributors.

Don Diego ate all of his meal, including dessert and poured some more wine. It had been a long hard day and tomorrow would be even harder and longer.

Life was good. Their net drug profits were running at over five million dollars per month and Latin Pizzaz was growing very rapidly and would grow even faster with the agreement he had put together in San Francisco earlier in the week.

He was lucky to have Paul Hastings as a partner. They had met during orientation of an MBA program that UCLA was offering; an intensive program that started in June after their undergraduate work had been completed and ran through August, fifteen months later.

Don Diego was not a "Don" in Mexico and in fact he had absolutely no claim whatsoever to trace his ancestors back to Spanish royalty. Don Diego was the illegitimate son of a merchant who owned an onyx quarry and a small factory that milled the stone into chess sets, ashtrays and other products. The merchant had acquired the business by marrying the daughter of the former owner. The daughter was neither beautiful nor fair of complexion but had given him two sons. The merchant had also taken a mistress and Diego was the product of that union. As an illegitimate son, he had no rights of inheritance and was mostly neglected by his father. When Diego had reached the age of fourteen, his father had given him a job cleaning up behind the plant workers and doing other odd jobs. Young Diego did everything he was asked and was soon doing milling, polishing and other more skillful jobs.

By the time Diego was sixteen, he could do just about every job in the factory. Diego's popularity with his coworkers and the office workers continued to grow, as did his knowledge of the business. His father finally realized that Diego had more intelligence, drive and ability than both of his natural sons together. He hired a tutor for Diego and put him in a prep school where the boy could prepare for college. At age 19, Diego was sent off to UCLA to study business administration. Four years later, he graduated and talked his father into financing another year at UCLA in order to pursue an MBA degree.

When Christmas break arrived, Paul accepted an invitation from Diego to spend Christmas in Mexico. During this vacation, Diego's father told them that he planned to retire in two years and that his older son would be in charge of world distribution and that the younger son would be in charge of operations.

"That," said Paul later in private as the two discussed this bit of news, "would put the company in bankruptcy within two years."

"We will have to deal with that," said Diego.

When spring break arrived, the two partners traveled to Europe to scout out the Italian onyx industry and the Swiss jewelry production industry. They also began to study women's fashions as they realized that stone-based jewelry, even when complemented with gold and silver, would never move in sufficient volumes to justify more than a small store in a mall.

They returned from Europe with the knowledge that they would need "a ton of cash" if they wanted to achieve their retail objectives.

Diego knew that Paul dealt cocaine and had done so throughout his college career. As a very popular football player, Paul had been a big man on campus and was welcomed at any campus party as well as other parties given by influential people. Paul normally completed his transactions in upscale bars, restaurants or at parties. Paul had also used a girlfriend or sometimes two assistants to complete a delivery. He would meet a customer at a party, give the person a hug, and introduce the person to his girlfriend. The girlfriend would do a kissy face with the customer and the money and drugs would change hands. Sometimes the girlfriend would then bump into Diego, who would take the money. A narc, watching this activity, would have trouble identifying just what went on.

The opportunity to increase their drug business occurred when Paul's supplier decided to retire and offered to sell Paul his business. "There are nine other guys besides you," said the supplier. "We cover the L.A. area and have a good share of the high roller recreational market. We don't deal with the street addicts who have to steal to support their habits."

When Paul told Diego about the opportunity and asked if Diego would take over his existing business, Diego said he would have to make up his mind overnight.

"Take as much time as you want," said Paul. "If you

say yes, it's forever. There ain't no looking back."

Diego had been dealing only a few months before his father retired and named his younger son as operations manager at the onyx works. About six months later, the younger son died in a fiery auto crash. Diego's father insisted that Diego take over the business. Diego demanded that his father stipulate in his will that Diego would inherit the entire business and that the older son would get a lifetime annuity sufficient to maintain himself in the status to which he had become accustomed. His father had agreed immediately. "Give him a title and an expense account so that he can pretend to be the big wheel, but you run the company the way it should be run."

Diego returned to Mexico and took charge of all company operations. He spent as much time in Europe as possible and hired two Italian managers to begin upgrading the onyx business and a Swiss jewelry production expert. Two years later, he named one of the Italians to be in charge of all of the Mexican operations and Diego returned to the U.S.

Paul Hastings continued to grow the cocaine business that he had taken over and to search for ways to reduce the risk of getting caught by the narcs.

It was Diego who made the breakthrough in improving security. As Diego continued to increase his international dealings, he began to understand how money was transferred from country to country. He met with the main person in the cartel who supplied their cocaine and worked out a deal to pay in advance for their shipments via wire transfers. Later when the partners had developed distributors to handle the retail end of the business, they further refined the system. The distributors first transferred the money to offshore accounts controlled by Don Diego and Hastings. The order would be placed with the drug cartel and payment would be transferred to the cartel's account. This reduced the risk to almost zero and over a period of years the two partners had taken over a huge portion of the West Coast drug business. With any luck, they would soon transfer all of their drug business to their distributors and their hands would be totally clean.

Chapter 13
Thursday A.M.
Jackson Hole, Wyoming

It was still early but Sam had been awake for hours, going over the details in his mind, trying to organize the things that he knew and the possible bad things that could go wrong.

Sam had called Jack Downs' office late Wednesday, hoping that Maria would answer. Jack answered the phone and was almost giddy as he told Sam about all of Don Diego's problems with the media and said that "your idea of the break in worked better than anyone ever dreamed. The media has been hyping it up all day long and Don Diego has been kept busy with the law-suit and the media questions about the cocaine that the cops found. He's scheduled to be on Channel 60 Thursday night defending himself and his company. I fully expect he'll be heading your way late tomorrow night but probably won't be there much before mid-night. Maria is out running some errands but she said tell you hello if you called and also tell you to be care-ful."

Sam was just about to call Harold's room when he

heard the knock on his door and went to open it. Harold came in and said, "There's news. Prince Valiant says that 'the solution' is anxious to hit the slopes and will arrive on his pumpkin just before the witching hour on Thursday. He also said to please respect the seniors and said that 'the object of your quest' is unhappy on the slopes. I confirmed receipt of his message."

"What do you make of that?"

"That she's here and struggling with whoever is holding her," said Harold.

"If he's that sure that she's here, why doesn't he send in the U.S. Marshals, FBI, local police and the U.S. Cavalry to rescue her?"

"I just plain don't know," said Harold. "I understand that he doesn't have the authority. The CIA is supposed to keep hands off of any domestic problem but that doesn't keep them from alerting all of the other agencies that do have the authority."

Sam thought for a moment and said, "He has to have a very good reason for not bringing in other authorities. You and he work for the same government agency but Jones has never called you or communicated with you except through this Prince Valiant rigamarole."

"That is absolutely correct, Sam. If he had called me, you would have been the first to know."

"What do you think he means when he says, 'respect for the elders'?

"Farmer Brown told me that there's a cook/house-keeper and a full time administrator in their sixties, who manages the farm and pays the bills."

"All right. We will continue to operate our plan. If Don Diego gets here at midnight tonight after the two bad days he has had, we just have to hope that he's too tired to hurt the girl tonight and we will be ready for him tomorrow morning."

"I came to the same conclusion," said Harold. "I'll check for messages throughout the day to make sure that nothing new comes up. Have you heard from Ellen?"

"Just that she and Bennie decided to stay over another day in Phoenix. The FBI told them yesterday that they had identified 'a person of interest' that they planned to question late yesterday and that she would call me today. Have you heard from the two Latinos?"

"Not yet. Let's get some breakfast and let them call us if they need us."

The call came about five minutes later. Lopez said, "Thank you very much, Sergeant Sam, for bringing us breakfast and offering to help us. A good non-com always takes care of his troops and we really appreciate you."

"Sorry, but the Captain and I slept late and we agreed that you two guys really didn't need any help or supervision. We have the utmost confidence that you will get the job done correctly."

"Actually," said Lopez, "we got a lot done yesterday afternoon, after you guys left and got out of our hair. We should be all finished by noon and we have a nice surprise for you. If you are not too tired and worn out from all the decisions you have to make, maybe you can bring us some lunch. And if it's not too much trouble, maybe you can bring something besides a happy meal. A hot beef or hot pork sandwich with potatoes, gravy and dressing would taste great."

"Count on it," said Sam. "It will be that or something better."

During breakfast Sam asked Harold how he had paid for the Hummer. "With a check for $9 thousand and that's only because the body was beat up and rusty."

"I'm a little concerned about that. Sooner or later someone's going to dig into the evidence and someone else is going to remember the Hummer with all the extra hardware on it and you're going to become a person of interest. I'm going to see if I can't hide that Hummer in Mississippi. The two guys can use a couple more days pay and I think I can talk a friend into making it disappear for awhile."

Sam had not seen Daryl Black since high school. They had been very good friends and he thought Daryl would help him out. He tried two different numbers for Daryl before calling information. This number produced a female voice who said Daryl was busy working horses but she would ask him to call back.

It wasn't long before his phone rang. It was Daryl, who opened up the conversation with, "Let's see. We graduated fourteen years ago and you finally get around to calling me. I suppose you want to apologize for leaving me in the on deck circle fourteen years ago. Sam, a Brownie Girl Scout could have slapped that last pitch into right field but you just stood there with the bat on your shoulder."

"You are absolutely right," said Sam. "And thanks for reminding me."

"I'm just kidding, Sam. What can I do for you?"

"I was wondering if you could hide an H-1 Hummer for me. Maybe just park it behind one of your sheds so it can't be seen from the road."

"Yeah, well I can understand why you would be ashamed of it. Were you drunk when you bought it?

You didn't steal it, did you Sam?"

"No, a good friend bought it for me. It's in his name and I don't want him to look stupid. Look, Daryl, you don't have to lie to anyone about it. If some sheriff asks you about it, you can tell him you are holding it for me. I'll be back home in a few weeks and take it off your hands."

"You gonna bring it down or send it down?"

"Two Latino guys who served with me in Afghanistan will bring it down."

"Okay, Sam. There's a motel in White Oak, Mississippi. Have them stay there and call me at three in the morning and I'll come meet them and lead them to my farm. Give them my home number."

"Thanks, Daryl. And one more time, you don't have to lie about it. If anyone asks just tell them it belongs to me."

"Come see me soon, Sam. I've got way more than two horses now and we'll go for another horse ride, buddy."

Sam relayed Lopez's message regarding lunch and suggested they go on out and see what the guys had come up with and then take them to lunch.

"Why not?" said Harold. "There's a truck stop not terribly far from the warehouse that should have some good food."

When they walked into the warehouse, they saw that a much shorter battering ram than the original design was protruding from the front of the vehicle.

"Are you sure it will work?" asked Sam.

"Positive," said Lopez. "We got a closer look at what was needed."

"How did you do that?"

"We went out there and walked up the steps slowly, counted them and measured them and then knocked on the door and asked if we could wash their windows."

At this point Sparky produced a flyer touting the services of "Mesa Window Cleaning Service". "We stopped at the World Express Copy Store and had them make up fifty copies of our flyers and went out there and knocked on the big oak doors. While we were waiting for them to answer we measured the steps and counted them and figured out just where the vehicle would be and what angle it would be at when it got close to the doors. I talked to them while Lopez was taking measurements. I was using very poor English with a fake Spanish accent so that Lopez had plenty of time to check it all out."

"Did you see them?"

"No, there's a speaker system. They were very rude and didn't even want to negotiate a price."

"Well, at least they didn't shoot you."

"No, but they said go away and don't ever come back. Very nasty people. Not at all nice."

Sam and Harold looked at the battering ram that was attached to the front of the vehicle. There were struts coming out from under the massive bumper and two more struts coming from under the hood. "The frame on these monsters comes up almost to the hood," said Lopez. "So we're attached to the frame at four points. The ram itself is attached at four points with a total of eight bolts. Sparky and I can do it by ourselves but it will be easier and faster with all four of us. Let's go through a dry run here in the warehouse and then we'll put it in the small bed in the rear. I have extra nuts, bolts and washers if we lose any."

Lopez proved to be correct in the ease with which they removed the heavy object, replaced it again and finally removed and placed it in the truck bed.

"Okay," said Sam. "After lunch you guys gather up your tools, get your rental stuff back where it goes and stick the scrap metal outside. Some scrounger will pick that up and get it to a scrap dealer. After that get some rest. Let's get some lunch now and later when I talk to Ellen I'll ask if she and Bennie can man the road blocks for the detour. If so, I'll need you guys to put something together."

Sam spent the afternoon going over his checklist and trying to think of what possibly could go wrong. He spoke with Ellen and Bennie, who were disappointed that the FBI's "person of interest" turned out to be of no interest whatsoever. As of four p.m., there had been no new messages from Prince Valiant. Sam knew from experience that something almost always goes wrong. Something unplanned usually happened. They would figure out how to dispose of the bodies of the bad guys. Injuries to one of his group would be harder to explain, especially a bullet wound. All four of the group understood that there was always a risk that someone would be injured or killed. They were no longer sheltered by the army and would have to answer to civilian authorities if anything went wrong. Sam had still made no decision about disposing of bodies. He didn't know how he would handle a wound or death to someone in his own crew. He knew he would pray as passionately as he could before he went to sleep.

Sam called Jack Downs' office and spoke to Maria for a few minutes, doing his best to sound upbeat and unworried. He spoke with Jack, who said there was no news other than the L.A. Times editorial page had a positive piece about the Latin Pizzaz Company and the economic benefits that the firm provided to the Los Angeles economy.

Bennie called and invited Sam to his room for a drink. When asked what he liked Sam replied, "Just a beer, please. Just one."

Sam knocked on Harold's door and asked if he had received the same invitation. The answer was yes and Sam's second question was "Were there more messages from Prince Valiant?" The answer to that question was no.

"Let's not discuss details," said Sam as they walked toward Bennie's room. "If Ellen asks, I intend to say that any gunfire will take place on the first floor and that our real estate lady has said there are no bedrooms or for that matter any rooms on the first floor that could be used to keep a hostage. We'll make no mention of that last message from the Prince. The FBI has essentially given up and we have no other place to look."

The cocktail hour went better than expected. Hannah's parents had apparently resigned themselves to the worse possible outcome. Ellen was especially nice to Sam and did ask what he thought the greatest danger was.

"That our plans to achieve a surprise will fail. If these plans work, it will go very well and there should be little risk to Hannah."

Sam declined a second drink as did Harold and the two excused themselves. Ellen left at the same time. She gave both the guys a hug and said, "Just do your best and don't take any more personal risk than you have to."

Chapter 14
D-Day

Hannah Lea had slept very little. She had awakened not long after she had first gone to sleep, faintly hearing voices. There was a new voice that she had not heard before and she assumed that was the "lover boy" the fat nurse had talked about. There was one other masculine voice that she didn't recall having heard before and she assumed that this was another security guard. She tried to control her breathing and tried to force herself to relax. She would need all of her strength because she intended to fight every step of the way. She heard voices for another half hour or so and then there was silence. She breathed a sigh of relief and tried to will herself to sleep. She prayed for strength and prayed that her death would not be drawn out. She had no illusions that her kidnappers would ever release her. She knew that death would be her only release.

Hannah Lea tossed and turned and finally went to sleep. She awoke desperately needing to go to the bathroom. She walked as fast as she could with her ankles bound with plastic cuffs. She sat on the toilet and opened the door to the cabinet under the vanity. It was there! A plunger with a wood handle about two feet long was in the cabinet. That had been her only hope to acquire a weapon. The day before she had systematically put almost an entire roll of paper in the toilet, hoping to create a plugged commode and it had worked. The fat nurse or more likely a security guard had left the plunger in the cabinet. Hannah decided to leave it there in the cabinet until the nurse was with her in the bathroom and turned her back toward Hannah. The nurse had told her yesterday that "we will get you a bubble bath when your lover boy gets here." Hannah didn't know how long she slept but awoke hearing activity in the nurse's bedroom. The nurse arrived with a bottle in her hand that Hannah assumed to be a bubble bath solution. As she shuffled toward the bathroom, she asked the nurse if she would remove her ankle cuffs as she was afraid she might fall in the bathtub. The nurse agreed, told her to "do her business" and shuffled off to get some scissors. Hannah sat on the pot, removed the plunger from the cabinet and unscrewed the handle. She slipped the handle under the slip that she wore and held it concealed against her leg. When the nurse removed the plastic cuffs, Hannah complained that the water was too hot, saying, "I can feel the heat from up here." The nurse muttered a curse and bent over to check the water. Hannah stood and swung the plunger handle as hard as she could, hitting the nurse across the back of the neck. The nurse screamed and tried to stand up. Hannah swung again from the other side, hitting the nurse across the bridge of her nose. The nurse tried one more time to stand up and was almost erect when Hannah hit her again. This time the nurse fell forward hitting her head on the bathtub water spigot and fell into the tub face first.

Hannah saw the waves of blood spreading through the water and was overcome with nausea. She turned and wretched into the toilet. There was very little in her stomach but she wretched again and then tried to pull the nurse out of the water. Hannah didn't have the strength to pull her out of the water and turned the water off. There were no more bubbles coming from the nurse's mouth. Hannah realized that she had killed a human being and wretched again. She started walking toward her room and then went back into the bathroom and felt in the nurse's housecoat pocket for the key ring. She went back to her room and started to collapse on her bed but instead turned and went to the door of the nurse's room and tried until she found the right key. She was looking for anything that she could use for a weapon but instead she saw the nurse's cell phone, picked it up and dialed her mother's cell number. Ellen answered on the second ring. All Hannah could do was sob. When she finally got control of herself, all she could say was, "I just killed a woman."

"Where are you, Hannah?"

"I think I'm in Jackson Hole," Hannah sobbed.

"Hannah, baby, we're just outside the house where you are. Can you turn your light off and on?"

Hannah flicked the light in the nurse's room off and on and Ellen said, "I saw a flicker. Is there another light that you can try?"

Hannah returned to her own room and flicked the light switch several times.

"That's it," said Ellen. "Leave your light on but get under your mattress. We're coming for you and you stay under your mattress until you hear my voice. I have to hang up now, baby."

Ellen called Sam. "Did you see that light flickering in the back of the house?"

"I did," said Sam.

"Hannah is in that room. I told her to get under a mattress."

Sam spoke into his radio phone, "Hannah is in the northeast corner of the house. When we enter the house it will be on our left."

Harold Brown was standing behind a small tree, leaning against it with his rifle cradled under his right arm and the barrel resting on a limb. He had been waiting for over half an hour. There had been decent light for a shot for several minutes now and he was getting anxious. There had been light in the room just to the left of the balcony for about twenty minutes now. Finally a figure ambled out onto the balcony and placed something on a table. Harold shifted into a firing position and looked through the scope. He couldn't make out what the person had put on the table but thought it might be a coffee pot under a fabric cozy.

Finally, another figure came out and poured some coffee into his cup and took a sip. Harold spoke into his radio phone, "Target in view." He took a deep breath, thumbed off the safety and let out part of the air. He centered the cross-hairs on the man's head and squeezed the trigger just as the man raised the cup to take a drink. The coffee cup disappeared and the man fell backwards. Harold watched for another few seconds and said, "Target is down; a good head shot, I think." Harold had been told to run for his truck immediately but he hesitated a second and saw a woman coming out on the balcony and then she turned and ran back inside.

Harold spoke again, "The target has been discovered. Go! Go!" and then Harold ran for his truck.

Sam wasted no time. The Hummer was running and Lopez gunned the engine, drove it out onto the main road and a few seconds later entered the driveway of the house, drove up the steps and didn't stop until the massive doors burst open. Sam and Lopez jumped out of the Hummer, rushed through the doors and were ready when two of the security guards appeared on the stair landing above them. Lopez and Sam both fired machine gun bursts at the same time. One of the security guards got off a burst of his own as he was falling. A ricochet bullet caught Sam in the lower left leg.

Lopez saw another security guard dash across the room toward what he assumed to be the downstairs guard station and said, "One heading your way, Sparky." Sparky took a knee, brought his carbine up and put three consecutive rounds into the third security guard. He then ran over and saw that this guard was very dead. He picked up the dead guard's weapon and spoke into his phone, "All secure outside." Sam spoke into his radio, "Sparky, come on in but guard that north entrance. Lopez, go upstairs and make sure it's secure. Where are you, Harold?"

"Just coming into the driveway."

"Come on in through the front doors. Ask the cook how many guards there were," Sam ordered.

"Three," came the answer.

"Okay," said Sam. "Check the basement," and added, "there's supposed to be a nurse somewhere."

Ellen's voice came over the radio, "Hannah said she killed the nurse."

"Get on in here, Ellen, and find your daughter. I need

a doctor," said Sam, as he looked at an ever widening pool of blood coming from his left leg.

Harold came through the doors, with Ellen right behind. He took Ellen's arm and helped her up the steps and around the bodies at the top landing.

"Where is my girl?" Ellen shouted at the older lady.

"Right through there," said the cook, "but the doors are locked."

"Open up, Hannah! It's okay, girl." The door opened and Hannah ran into her mother's arms sobbing.

Sam was still sitting on the floor downstairs. "Somebody please bring me a couple of towels and something to twist with before I bleed to death."

The old man, the caretaker, came downstairs with two towels and a long screwdriver. He put a small folded cloth over the wound, took two wraps with the other towel and began twisting with the screwdriver. The old man spoke quietly to Sam. "I talked to Jones. He's on his way here with a doctor and a cleanup crew."

"Well, at least there's that, why in hell didn't he come a little earlier and give us a hand with the really dirty work?"

Chapter 15
Prince Valiant to the Rescue

Sparky and Lopez returned to where Sam was sitting on the floor and asked how he was doing.

"Terrible. It's still bleeding and it's about as painful as anything I've ever felt. You guys get the vehicles around back and push the big doors closed if you can."

The two Latinos returned from moving the vehicles and Lopez said, "We have company."

Jones, aka Prince Valiant, appeared with four other men, one of whom carried a doctor's case. "Is there a bed or a cot on this level?" asked the doctor.

"There's a rollaway in the pantry behind the kitchen," said the housekeeper.

"Bring that and bring me a chair and get me a good lamp," the doctor ordered.

Jones had completed his tour of the house and said, "You need four body bags?"

"Five," said Sam. "The nurse is upstairs."

The doctor cut off the lower pants leg from Sam and said, "That is a very nasty wound. You need a hospital and a surgeon. The bleeding is stopped and we'll get you to a hospital."

"We'll take them to San Luis Obispo," said Jones.

"Why so far away?" asked Ellen, who had appeared with Hannah and Bennie.

"It's only an hour away on my Gulfstream," said Jones. "And they'll be ready for both Sam and Hannah."

The doctor had led Hannah a few steps away and was talking to her in low tones. Hannah was shaking her head, no she had not been raped but she had been given injections of a powerful drug and she had been slapped, kicked, and had suffered from diarrhea and vomiting and felt very weak.

The doctor returned and told Ellen that Hannah should definitely go to the special clinic in California." They are better equipped to make sure that Hannah isn't suffering from any virus that might come from a contaminated needle."

"Get them on the plane and we'll get out of here as soon as possible," said Jones. He asked the doctor if Sam needed an ambulance to get to the plane.

"No," said the doctor. "The Yukon will be fine."

"Get 'em on the plane, I'm right behind you as soon as I get the clean-up crew going. What was that vehicle I saw moving around back?" Jones asked Sam.

"An H-1 Hummer with a battering ram," said Sam. "That's how we got through the front doors. I'm going to send it to Mississippi."

"I have a better idea," said Jones. "I'll send it to a scrap dealer in Omaha who can make it disappear totally. The bodies will all be cremated and the ashes disposed of. Leave Brown with me and he can help me organize the clean-up. We'll put him on a plane for Oklahoma City later."

"Maybe Bennie can give Harold a ride to Oak City,"

said Sam as two of the clean up guys began to carry him out the side door.

Jones turned his attention to Brown and asked, "What was your cover for being here?"

"Helping my wealthy friend, Sam, locate a nice house to buy."

"How about the two Latinos out back?"

"They were never here. They stayed in a motel twenty miles away."

"What other tracks did you leave?"

"None. I had Sparky and Lopez rent the warehouse over in Rockville and they paid cash for the warehouse. There was no rental agreement to sign."

"Okay," said Jones. "Assume the owner has another key and don't worry about it. Look, if anyone asks about the Hummer, tell them you bought it for me. I'll handle that. We're going to sanitize this place and close it up. In a year or so, when the taxes aren't paid, the county or city will begin proceedings. It could be two or three years before that is settled."

Jones turned to the caretaker and said, "Bring all of the cash from the safe and something to use for a bill of sale."

"Harold, I'm going to give you two hundred thousand for you to give to Sam to reimburse him for all his expenses in this project. He can divide it up however he wants. I'm going to write out a bill of sale marked paid to Farmer Brown for the cattle out there. Can you take that bill of sale to him?"

"Yes, but I'm going to tell him to save me a feisty little bull calf. I need to talk to Sparky and Lopez. They have a rental car from California that they need to take back along with our arsenal. Lopez works for a gun dealer in San Diego and they can handle that. Bennie and I will drop off the bill of sale and move on out. I'll turn in the rented truck at the airport."

"That should close the loop," said Jones. "I think the tracks are all wiped out. I'll look you up next time you're in Washington and tell you the rest of the story. You guys did a hell of a job."

"Sam was our honcho; he deserves the credit and I would appreciate if you could explain to Sam your reasons for leaving us on our own and not sending in the cavalry to do what we did."

"I'll do that. Right now I have to catch up with him."

Jones boarded the Gulfstream and about five minutes later they were airborne. Sam was too sedated to engage in conversation. He felt weak and nauseous and leaned back in his seat. There was one spare jump seat that the doctor had used to prop up Sam's injured leg. The doctor continued to check Sam's vital signs from time to time but let him doze.

Hannah Lea was munching on some cookies and sipping a soft drink, while leaning her head on her mother's shoulder.

Jones assessed the situation and decided he would talk to them later. Sam's dozing turned into heavy sleep punctuated with an occasional snore. Jones decided to let mother and daughter continue to cuddle until he heard the engines being throttled back and the plane began a slow descent. Jones excused himself and asked if Hannah could answer a couple of questions. Hannah nodded her head and Jones showed her a picture of Paul Hastings. "Is this the man who kidnapped you?"

"Yes!" said Hannah.

"You were then driven to L.A. and put on a plane

with the nurse and a security guard and flown to Jackson Hole. Is that correct? Do you know how many drug injections you were given?"

"Four or five, I think," said Hannah. "I fought them as hard as I could."

"The most important thing for you right now is to make sure those needles weren't tainted and that you haven't been exposed to something worse than heroin or cocaine. This hospital you're going to can determine that and that's why I insisted that you come here. Sam also will get the best treatment available here. Don't breathe a word about this conversation or about me. Hannah will be admitted under the name of Jane Smith. Any questions about Hannah's real name or anything else should be answered with the words, "absolutely no comment." Paul Hastings won't be arrested until later today and I may spend two days debriefing him. After that, I'll come back and give you, Sam, and Ellen a complete explanation." Jones then asked the pilot if it was okay to take a flash picture of Hannah. The pilot asked if he could wait until the plane was on the ground.

Chapter 16
The Roundup Begins

Paul Hastings returned to LAX and signed the bill for his charter plane. It had been a very hectic two days and he had met with some resistance from his distributors but overall his two-day marathon had gone very well. By the end of the week-end all of the distributors should have transitioned into a more defensive mode with considerably less risk. On Sunday he would meet with a top cartel honcho in Baja, Mexico and let them know what was going on. The cartel trusted him and he would keep them informed. Right now he was very tired and needed to relax.

He walked to his Yukon and glanced at the boxy German camper vehicle parked next to it. It was a very efficient diesel-powered vehicle and he had considered buying one himself. Paul unlocked his car and started to step in when he felt a very sharp stinging pain in the back of his neck. His knees weakened and he slipped to the pavement. Paul soon woke up because someone was spraying water on his face and wiping it off with a towel. He could move neither his hands nor his feet and soon realized that he was sitting inside the German built SUV.

"We moved to a more isolated area while you were asleep, so you can yell and scream all you want and that will just make me angry and uncooperative. My name is Jones and I'm depending on you to do the cooperating because I hold all the aces. Let me first get you up to date, Mr. Hastings. Here is a picture of a young woman holding a picture of you. I have a signed statement from her that you picked her up bodily in front of her apartment in Mesa, Arizona, on Wednesday, nine days ago. Then you drove her across a state line to L.A. and had her flown to still another state, Wyoming."

"Let's see what else we have here. This is a picture of your Yukon. It has your license plate number and you can see Camelback Mountain in the background. That puts your vehicle in the Phoenix area on the day of the kidnapping."

"Oh yes, here is a copy of a court order authorizing the listening device we installed in Don Diego's hotel apartment last Wednesday and it's signed by a federal judge. The last man through on your sweeping crew actually works for me. That was a very good conversation to hear because you and Don Diego talked in detail about your drug distributors and also you discussed the kidnapped woman."

"The roundup of your distributors and dealers started about two minutes after you said goodbye to your guy in Las Vegas. We have about one hundred DEA, FBI, state police and other guys participating in this roundup. You know what's really nice, Paul? This late on Friday we don't really have to report any of this until the next workday, which is Monday. You and I can spend the entire glorious week-end bonding together."

"Who is the guy you are meeting with on Sunday in Baja? That's okay, Paul, you can tell me later. We have so much we can talk about, don't we?"

"Some more big news will be released Monday or it might leak out before and that's that Don Diego may have absconded to Mexico with three bodyguards and a nurse. There was a 'mystery plane' that landed at the Jackson Hole airport about the same time Don Diego's personal plane landed. Some time after midnight that same plane took off for Mexico City. Don Diego isn't answering his phone and nobody is answering the phone or opening the doors at his Jackson Hole mansion. It's a huge mystery."

"I'm not telling you jack," said Paul.

"Well you may not," said Jones. "But you know I can do anything I want to with you between now and Monday and after that I can haul you around to nine states and keep you in the worst possible jails in the western U.S. You know there's no bail available for kidnapping and transporting someone across state lines."

"You can't hold me over the weekend without allowing me access to a lawyer."

"Actually, I can," said Jones. "I can shoot your ass full of drugs, like you tried to do to the girl in Jackson Hole. I can do anything I want to including dropping you out of a helicopter into the Pacific."

"Here's what we're going to negotiate, Paul. I want account numbers, routing numbers, and names of banks, transfer agents, and everything else you can tell me about your drug finances and who you deal with. If you cooperate fully with me, you can spend the rest of your life in a nice comfy cupcake, country club type prison. If you don't, you may not live through the weekend. Your decision."

"Take him out to the desert and let him go to the bathroom in the sand but keep him tied up. If he tries to escape, shoot him as many times as you think necessary."

Jones drove to his apartment, showered, and put a steak on his grill. He made a salad to go with it and had just sat down to watch a Dodgers game when his phone rang. "Hastings wants to talk."

"What made him change his mind?"

"He's afraid of rattlesnakes in the desert."

"I didn't think he was afraid of anything," said Jones. "Okay, get you a double bed motel room out that way. Keep him chained to a bed and keep two guns pointed at him all night. Make sure he understands that the prison will be maximum security but low density. There will be lots of shuffleboard, card games, etc. Also make sure he knows that he'll accept the court appointed attorney that we choose to defend him. I'll call you in the morning and let you know where we'll meet. I'll also have an officer with me who understands money transfers and international laws regarding the transfer of money."

It was Tuesday afternoon before Jones could get away from L.A. and fly back to San Luis Obispo. He found Hannah in the employees' recreation room playing a mean game of ping pong with an Oriental hospital employee. Ellen was watching her daughter intently. Jones asked Ellen if she would bring Hannah Lea to Sam's room when the ping pong match was over.

Jones found Sam's room where Sam and an attractive Latin woman were poring over brochures of large travel coaches, at least forty feet long. "I'm ordering it from a dealer in Jackson, Mississippi, but it will be delivered out here. Maria has agreed to be my full time chauffeur," said Sam.

"I didn't agree yet," said Maria. "But I'm considering it."

"How's the leg?" asked Jones.

"It's fine," said Sam.

"It is not fine," Maria said. "They had to do a bone graft and some other major repairs and Sam will be here at least another week and he won't be able to walk without crutches for three or four weeks."

"Ellen and Hannah will be here shortly and I'll tell you all why I didn't call in the cavalry to rescue Hannah. Sam, is Maria familiar with what has been going on?"

"Oh yes," said Sam. "Maria has worked for Jack Downs Detective Agency for several years and she knows all about Don Diego and Paul Hastings."

"I thought I had heard that voice before," said Jones. "But we had never met."

When Ellen and Hannah entered the room, Jones began to talk. "I'm a twenty-year veteran of the CIA but was recently selected to do a special project 'by order of the President'. A Presidential Order stipulates that all government agencies are required to cooperate with me and supply whatever information or assets I request within reason. I worked mainly with the Treasury Department who were questioning some of the money transfers being made by Don Diego, Paul Hastings, and the chief financial officer of the Latin Pizzaz Corporation. I also worked with the Drug Enforcement Agency which was unable to determine just how the drug cartel was able to make its deliveries and how they were getting paid. Just recently we were able to determine that payment was being made by international transfers and we began to identify some of the distributors as well as some of the dealers."

"We were able to put everything together this weekend and we put a hold on over two billion dollars from the accounts of Hastings, Don Diego, ten major West Coast distributors, and about forty street and volume dealers. There'll be more arrests as these guys begin to sing. Most of these arrests occurred between Friday afternoon and early this morning."

"Now you can understand why we didn't call in the cavalry to rescue Hannah and arrest Don Diego. Number one, that would have been as risky or riskier to Hannah than leaving it in the hands of Sam, Harold Brown, and their two assistants. Number two, an arrest or a shooting of Don Diego would have totally blown what we accomplished this weekend and I could not let that happen. Number three, there's no way I was going to leave Hannah Lea in the clutches of Don Diego for the entire weekend. Before I allowed that to happen, I would go in myself with the four guys I had with me.

"The reason I didn't use my own crew is that Sam's gang was more qualified. I requested and read both Sam's and Harold's service records and decided they were more qualified than my crew. My crew and I became the backup crew. The story about Don Diego escaping to Mexico on the 'mystery' charter plane has been accepted by the media. That may have been my one flash of brilliance in this entire episode. I thought of that on Thursday afternoon and was able to route a plane through Jackson Hole. Creating an escape for Don Diego solves a lot of problems!"

"The FBI reported that Hannah Lea was released by

her kidnappers and was recuperating in a private clinic. My suggestion is that Hannah return home with her mother, where she'll have a better chance to recover in an atmosphere more private. We all need to understand that there are four attorneys, including myself, who could risk disbarment if all the facts came out. Ellen really doesn't want people to know that she financed a fire in a crowded department store. Hannah doesn't want to go through life recounting her fight with the nurse. The caretaker couple has entered the witness protection program. Just remember the three key words, "absolutely no comment." I wish all of you the very best," said Jones as he started for the door.

Sam held out his hand to Jones and said, "Thanks for your help." Ellen and Hannah also shook Jones' hand as he walked out the door.

"Hey, Hannah Lea, when is your fishing trip to Oregon?" asked Sam.

"How did you know about that?"

"Your dad told me."

"It's late next month. Did you want to come fish with us?"

"No thanks, but I want to see the country and Maria and I could arrange to be there on our way North. Did you ever tell your mom about your fishing trip?"

"No, I don't think so," said Hannah. Ellen shook her head no also.

"Well, your mother dreamed that she was fly fishing with you. She dreamed that one night last week when things were at their darkest and I think it was a sign. A sign that should be celebrated and remembered."

"I'll have to think about that," said Hannah Lea. "But you are certainly welcome to come see us in Oregon."

After Ellen and Hannah Lea left, Sam asked Maria, "Did she think her parents would prefer them to be married or just shacked up?"

"Sam! You know the answer to that."

"Well call them and give them two weeks to call a crowd and let's get it done before I get too old."

Maria couldn't help laughing but said, "That isn't a very romantic proposal."

"Well, I'm certainly not able to get down on my knees and propose properly. I think Henry would understand."

"Henry would agree with anything you say, Sam. But Mother and I will make all the important decisions."

"I certainly hope so. I'm not going to discuss the color of the tablecloth and napkins for the wedding dinner."

"Do you want to set a limit on how much we spend?'

"No. Do whatever you want. I like nice and classy but not too ostentatious. If that's the right word."

Maria put part of her weight on the narrow bed and kissed Sam. "I think we'll be very happy. Do you have any other orders?"

"Yes, call Jack Downs and tell him to find a replacement for you. I told him over a week ago and he didn't believe me. It's his own fault. Also check with the person in charge of rooms here and see if they have a room with a queen size hospital bed."

"You know the answer to that Sam. Think about nice peaceful things and try to get some sleep."

Sam pushed the button to call a nurse and asked for a pain pill. He opened the drawer of his bedside stand and looked at the date on his watch. He had been discharged from the army not quite three weeks ago. When he thought about Maria, the pain in his leg was considerably less. He thought about Alabama. Maybe if he treated Maria really well, the stupid, ungrateful dog would show him a little love. Sam then realized it was Maria who had insisted that he leave the dog with her. You don't suppose dogs have some sort of power? Nah, that's not possible, or is it?

Epilogue

Sam and Henry had been banished from the wedding planning discussion. Henry's suggestion that he would order two kegs of "his wine" was quickly vetoed by Maria's mother. Sam's suggestion that Alabama would make a good ring bearer was scornfully nixed by Maria. When Henry suggested that he and Sam should check out the Dodgers game, both women agreed instantly.

Henry turned on the TV and asked Sam if he would like a glass of wine. Sam said, "No thanks," because Maria didn't want him drinking wine while walking on crutches. Henry poured himself a glass of wine and poured a small amount into a glass for Sam. "Take a small sip of the wine and rub some more on your lips," said Henry. "You don't ever want to give a Latin woman too many victories or you'll lose control of your life. It's part of their DNA."

Sam laughed and said he would try to remember that advice. His leg was almost free of pain and he was anxious to get the wedding over with and to start a new life with Maria.

Bennie had called two days before and said that an Atlanta City judge had issued a continuance in the case against James Dawson, the young man who had attempted to rob the Atlanta C-Store. The young man himself had called Sam the day before and thanked him profusely for his help in getting him into a rehab clinic.

Sam had spoken twice with Hannah Lea. She had reserved a room in Oregon for Sam and Maria. Hannah told Sam that she was going to return to Arizona after the fishing vacation in Oregon. First up would be a three day hike in the Grand Canyon with her hiking friends. Next she would get serious about passing the Arizona bar exam. She had also decided which law firm she was going to join and that she would make a career in criminal law. Her ultimate goal was to be a prosecuting attorney and put bad guys in prison.

Ben Emison   Jerry Branscum

About the Authors

Ben Emison and Jerry Branscum were friends and class-mates from third grade through high school and then lost touch for the next fifty years.

Jerry did well in math and literature, while Ben excelled in sports. Their daydreams were similar, but Ben's all took place on the back of a horse.

Ben continues to enjoy a very successful career in the horse business, and Jerry had a successful business career that included living in Europe and extended travel in Latin America.

Ben is what you might call a slow writer, as he start-ed this book in the late nineties. A decade later and a reunion with a classmate, Jerry Branscum, the two fin-ished the book. Ben has four other books lying in state, waiting to be finished.